# FINDING PERFECTION

## CLUB PRIVÉ 6

### M. S. PARKER

BELMONTE PUBLISHING, LLC

Copyright © 2016 Belmonte Publishing LLC

Published by Belmonte Publishing LLC

# READING ORDER

Thank you so much for reading the Club Privé series. If you'd like to read the complete series, I recommend reading them in this order:

# ONE

## KRISSY

It seemed like more than a year since I'd been in New York, not a little less than one. For six years, this city had been my home. The three women I'd met here had become more of a family to me than my own mother and father. Dena and Leslie stood with me now as we waited for the fourth member of our group to appear. Carrie and her fiancé, Gavin, were the reason my own boyfriend, DeVon, and I had flown in from LA. Not only were Carrie and Gavin officially announcing their engagement, but it was also the re-opening of their club, the place where they'd had their first date. Well, sort of. The story of their relationship was the only one I knew that was even crazier than how DeVon and I had come together. The two of them had been through a lot and they deserved this celebration.

"There." DeVon's voice sent a shiver through me even though there wasn't anything sexual about the word or his intensions. His hand on my back sent heat through me that had nothing to do with the press of bodies all around us.

I followed where he pointed and saw the person I'd been looking for. I grinned and shouted her name as I made my way through the crowd towards my friend. When I'd first met her at

Columbia, she'd been much quieter and definitely less well-dressed. She was always beautiful, but her time with Gavin had given her the confidence to show the person I'd always known her to be.

We'd been roommates since freshman year and being apart for this long hadn't been easy. Of course, we'd both made new friends and found the paths our lives were meant to take, but that didn't mean we hadn't missed each other. The thing about being so close, the two of us picked up right where we'd left off. After a while, Dena and Leslie chose partners from their many admirers and moved off to dance. Gavin and Carrie headed off somewhere – I assumed to visit the private room she'd told me about the club having. And I definitely didn't blame her. If I had a hot guy and a private sex playroom, I'd spend as much time in there as possible. Well, at least I had one half of that equation here.

I looked up at DeVon. "Shall we dance?" I held out my hand.

He smiled at me, a slow, sensual smile that tightened things low inside me. That was the kind of smile I'd learned held the promise of great things to come. When DeVon and I had first been doing this little back-and-forth thing where we tried to deny how we felt about each other, he'd said that he didn't dance. When asked why by one of our mutual friends, he'd said it was because he'd never found the right partner.

He slid his hand into mine and the two of us moved onto the dance floor. His hand slid up my bare arm and then down to the small of my back. He pulled me tight against him until our bodies were pressed together intimately. If we'd been at a normal dance club, it might've been almost obscene, the way we began to move together, but here, everything was a precursor to sex. Well, except for the actual sex that I assumed was happening in the more dimly lit parts of the club.

"That dress looks amazing." DeVon pressed his mouth against my ear. The hand on my back moved down to my ass. "But I don't like it."

I turned my head enough to give him a puzzled look.

"Too many men in here are wondering if you could possibly look as good without it as you do with it." His hand slid lower and the tips of his fingers brushed against the tops of my thighs.

I'd specifically chosen this dress because it wasn't one I could wear to a function back home – when had I started referring to LA as home instead of New York? – and the re-opening of a sex club had seemed like the perfect fit for it. It was simple in the sense that it was plain white, without any fancy stitching or cuts, but no one would describe the dress as boring. At least not the way I was wearing it. Carrie would've called the dress one of my "barely there" outfits.

"There are just as many women looking at you," I countered. And it wasn't just women. I saw more than a few men looking our way who weren't checking me out.

"Well, if people are looking..." DeVon's Italian accent thickened the way it always did when he was angry or aroused. "Maybe we should give them something to look at."

I was wearing my favorite heels, which put me close enough to DeVon's over-six-feet frame that all I had to do was tilt my head for our faces to be only an inch apart. I saw the heat in his eyes and then his mouth was coming down on mine. Electricity zinged through me as his tongue darted into my mouth, tasting of the champagne we'd been drinking. I wrapped my arms around his neck and buried my fingers in his wavy, black hair. He slid his hand under my dress, squeezing my ass even as his action pushed the hem up enough to flash some flesh at the people around us. The idea that men were ogling my ass as DeVon fondled it made me writhe against him, less of a dance now than something even more primal.

I bit down on DeVon's bottom lip, then sucked it into my mouth, reveling in the growl I felt reverberating through his chest. His mouth moved down my jaw even as his free hand tangled in the hair I'd left down to cascade over my shoulders. With a tug that sent a jolt straight through me, he yanked my head to the side and kissed his way down my neck.

I dug my nails into his shoulders as he sucked the tender skin of my throat into his mouth. Ever since we'd gone public with our relationship, he'd been enjoying leaving hickeys and bite marks in visible places. My neck. Collarbone. The tops of my breasts. My eyelids fluttered as DeVon sucked on my neck, each pull making me even more wet.

He slid his hand down my leg and pulled it up, hooking it around his hip. I ignored the fact that my skirt was gathering up around my waist and flashing my white thong. All I cared about was the way DeVon's cock was now rubbing against me just right.

"Do you think you can get off like this?" DeVon asked as he sucked my earlobe into his mouth. He ground his pelvis against me and I moaned. "Dancing with all these people around us, knowing that all they have to do is look and they'll see your firm ass in those tiny little panties."

It hit me then. He wasn't going to let this go until I came. A thrill ran through me. I wasn't an exhibitionist. Not in a true sense where I'd want people watching me have sex, like on a stage or someone in my room, but this was different. Aside from the fact that I was actually clothed, the club wasn't brightly lit. People would see mostly shadows, the suggestion of what we were doing. If they were paying attention to us in the first place. People were probably more interested in their own partners.

Still, it turned me on, knowing people could watch at least a bit while DeVon and I danced.

He covered my mouth with his, the kiss hard and demanding. All of the desire I could feel in his body, the tension in his arms, how hard his cock was as it pressed against me, he poured all of it into that kiss. His tongue thrust into my mouth, exploring every inch of it. I moaned as I writhed against him, the fabric providing exquisite friction against my clit. We'd been together for almost a year and it was still fireworks every time we touched.

His fingers tightened in my hair, sending little pinpricks of pain and pleasure into my scalp. He tore his mouth away from mine and our eyes met. The love and desire that burned there only made me want to come more. I loved being able to do what he asked. What he commanded. I loved the expression on his face when I obeyed.

"Come, Ms. Jensen."

I smiled as I remembered how our first time together, he'd used my last name rather than my first, as if it could put a distance between us. It hadn't worked even then.

"Come for me, baby." His hand tightened on my hip, fingers digging into flesh, the extra pressure exactly what I needed.

I groaned, biting my bottom lip to hold back the cry that wanted to escape. I shuddered as I came and DeVon released my leg. I put my foot on the floor, but it was DeVon's arms that held me steady, kept us moving to the music until the strength returned to my legs. Once I could stand on my own, I reached down and took his hand, moving us off of the dance floor. I waved at Dena and Leslie as we passed, but I didn't stop. I'd spend time with them tomorrow. As for Carrie and Gavin, I wasn't going to waste my time looking for them. I knew they were busy. And once DeVon and I got back to our hotel, I intended to be just as busy.

# TWO
## KRISSY

"You packed the handcuffs?" I raised an eyebrow. I wasn't sure why I was surprised. I'd been on several trips with DeVon in the time we'd been together and he believed in the Boy Scout motto of always being prepared. I just doubted whoever had come up with that motto had been thinking of sex toys at the time.

DeVon and I had been all over each other from the moment we'd gotten into the town car Gavin had commissioned for us for the weekend. Before we'd gone more than a couple yards, DeVon had me stretched out on the seat and was pulling off my panties. I'd spared a moment to glance at the tinted window between us and the driver, but then DeVon had pushed my legs up so that my feet were flat on the seat – or at least as flat as they could be in heels – and I'd known what was coming next.

"Shh," DeVon cautioned. "I don't know how soundproofed it is back here."

I'd considered glaring at him, but then he'd pressed his mouth against the inside of my thigh, sucking and nipping at the tender skin there until I'd been fighting back moans. The first time he'd ever marked me, it had been in that same spot, a place where no one from work would've been able to see it since

Mirage had strict no-fraternization policies at the time. Things had changed since DeVon and I had started dating.

"I wonder how many times I can make you come before we get to the hotel?" he'd asked just before burying his face between my legs.

Thanks to some traffic, the answer had turned out to be three times. Before I'd met DeVon, that would've been a record for a whole night with a lover. Since we'd gotten together, the four orgasms I'd had so far tonight had become about average. And I'd gotten the impression that tonight wasn't going to be average.

He'd had to help me walk into the hotel and I'd been pretty sure the people we'd passed had thought I was drunk. I hadn't cared what they thought, as long as they hadn't realized that my panties had been in DeVon's pocket and that, despite DeVon's very attentive tongue, the insides of my thighs had been dripping.

Now, we were in our room, standing next to our king-sized bed, and DeVon was holding up a pair of handcuffs and giving me that wicked grin of his that said I was going to be sore tomorrow. I held out my hands in the universal sign for 'cuff me, Officer. I've been naughty.'

"Strip." His voice held that authoritative note that had always twisted something inside me.

First went the shoes. Then, I grabbed the hem of my dress and pulled it over my head in one quick gesture, leaving me in just a strapless bra, the same white lace as the panties in his pocket. I gave him a moment to appreciate the view and then tossed the bra on the floor, too. With a sly grin, I ran my hands up my sides and cupped my breasts. They weren't overly large, but they weren't small either, just a bit above average. DeVon's eyes narrowed as I caressed my breasts, my fingers making circles around my nipples until they hardened into little bullet points.

"Did I say you could touch yourself?" He took a step towards me and I shivered in anticipation.

When I'd first met DeVon, I'd thought he'd been a control freak, wanting nothing more than to boss women around into pleasuring him. I'd ended up realizing that hadn't been the case. He enjoyed domination and I definitely enjoyed submitting to him, but what made us work was that I wasn't the traditional definition of a Sub. Not in the BDSM world. I liked pushing back...and he liked it when I did. What made us so good for each other was that we understood the other's needs and knew exactly how to fill them.

"No, Sir." I gave my nipples a light pinch and watched DeVon's eyes darken to almost black.

He reached out and took one of my wrists. Cool metal brushed my skin as he clicked one side of the handcuffs into place. Immediately, I knew that these weren't the flimsy trick ones that magicians used on their assistants. These were the real thing. Only one way out and that was the key DeVon set on the table next to the bed before reaching for my other hand.

He paused for a moment, a thoughtful expression on his face. I didn't say anything, letting him make whatever decision it was he was making. After a moment, he locked my hands in front of me and then took a step back. Slowly, he peeled off the fitted t-shirt he was wearing, revealing a long, lean torso with defined muscles beneath tanned skin. He was tall, with broad shoulders, but not quite as muscular as, say, Gavin. But like my friend's fiancé, DeVon had a strength and power to him that went beyond build. He was physically intimidating, but it was truly his charisma and personality that made people listen to him.

He unbuttoned his jeans and pulled the zipper down, but

didn't take them off. He left them open, revealing a thin trail of black curls that ran from his belly button down to disappear between the folds of fabric.

I realized, with a jolt of desire, that he wasn't wearing anything under his jeans. I bit my lip. If I'd known that, I would've had my hand down his pants and around his cock back at the club.

He reached into the bag he'd taken the handcuffs out of and what came out next made my mouth go dry.

The leather belt was wide, definitely too wide to be fashionable. Not that DeVon really wore belts unless he had something like this in mind. Those were all stylish, and much thinner, which meant they hurt more. Wide belts were more like hands, spreading the sensations over a distance.

This was something that I hadn't known before I'd met him.

"Turn around."

I stayed where I was for a moment, holding his gaze, and then I did as I was told. I spread my legs shoulder-width apart, but stayed straight, not knowing how else he wanted me positioned. Over the past few months, he'd spanked me with his hand and used a crop on me. The belt had been a recent addition, though he still only kept to my ass. I knew some women – including former lovers of his – had wanted him to whip their backs and breasts. Some had even wanted their pussies whipped. I'd always liked things a bit rough, but he was still easing me into a lot of the kinkier things he enjoyed. My ass throbbed at the memory of the first time he'd taken me there. I'd slept with my fair share of men and I'd never been close to a prude, but DeVon had been my first for quite a few things.

"Hands on the bed."

It was a bit awkward with the handcuffs, but I balanced myself on my hands and waited.

The first blow was across both cheeks, barely enough to

sting. The second was harder, heat spreading across my skin. Three and four came quick together and I gasped. The fifth made me cry out as it caught me across the lower part of my ass, the leather almost, but not quite, brushing against my pussy

"Move to your elbows."

I hesitated and leather cracked against my skin again. I did as I was told, suddenly aware of how much this position exposed my pussy as well as my ass.

The belt came down again, this time, curling around my hips, the center of it lightly connecting with my lower lips. My entire body jerked. It hadn't hurt. Not exactly. It was a sharp sensation, unlike anything I'd felt there before. When he repeated the same strike, I made a strangled sound that I wasn't sure was a protest, but I didn't know if it was a plea to continue, either. My brain scrambled to make sense of everything I was feeling.

When my legs were trembling and my body was torn between pain and pleasure, only then did he finally stop. My ass felt like it was on fire. He hadn't quite taken me to the bruising point, but sitting tomorrow was going to be a real bitch.

"That's my girl." He leaned over me and pressed his lips against my spine.

I sighed as his mouth began to make its way down my back, his tongue tracing patterns across my skin. When his hands slid over my ass, I whimpered, a shudder running through my entire body. His touch was gentle, but my skin was so sensitive that even the slightest touch was felt. Then his tongue was soothing my pussy.

I moaned as his mouth moved up. Another new thing I'd been on the giving and receiving end of recently. When we'd gotten ready for tonight, DeVon had given me a suggestion that I was now glad I'd followed. The tip of his tongue teased at my asshole, lightly moving over it even as he slid a finger into my pussy. The duel sensations began to pull me towards yet another climax. When he pushed a second finger into me, I squeezed my eyes shut as the first ripple of orgasmic pleasure washed over me. He twisted his fingers, his knuckles rubbing against my g-spot.

As I began to come, he pulled his mouth away, focusing on pumping his fingers into me, forcing my climax harder and higher. My knees bent and I writhed on his hand, unsure if I was trying to get away or get more of him inside me. Then his hand was gone and my legs almost gave out.

The smell of mint filled the air and I heard liquid being spat into the trashcan. A moment later, DeVon used my hair to pull me upright and turn my face towards him. I could taste mouthwash as he kissed me. It was teeth and tongue, as rough as his previous treatment had been, and my pussy dripped with my arousal.

"I was going to fuck your ass from behind," he said as he pulled away.

I shivered, remembering how intense that first experience had been, the way he'd stretched me, filled me. I could only imagine how it would feel combined with his hips slapping against my overheated and already sore skin.

"But I changed my mind." He released me so suddenly that I almost fell.

By the time I regained my balance, he was already on the bed, his long body stretched out, cock jutting up in the air, thick and swollen.

"I want to watch those beautiful tits of yours bounce while you ride me." He crooked his finger at me and motioned me forward. "And you're going to make yourself come at least one more time before I do."

I climbed onto the bed, waiting for the rest. He never gave me something so easy. My entire body was like a live wire, every nerve burning. It wouldn't take much for me to get off again.

"But you can't touch your clit."

Damn him.

I glared at him as I awkwardly swung a leg over his waist. I put my hands on his stomach, flexing my fingers until my nails dug into his skin. He hissed, his hands moving to grip my thighs. He pulled me forward until his cock bumped against my pussy. I reached beneath me to position him at my entrance, but I didn't lower myself onto him. Not yet. I slid just the head inside, teasing him with the tight heat he knew was waiting for him.

"Do you think you're in charge, Ms. Jensen?" His question was half-teasing. It had been what he'd asked me the first time we'd slept together, letting me know in no uncertain terms who was in control.

"I don't know, Mr. Ricci," I teased right back. "From where I'm sitting, it sure seems like it."

His hands moved up to my breasts. I gasped as he squeezed them, then cried out when his fingers began to work on my nipples. I kept my hands on his stomach as I struggled to stay upright. He twisted and pulled, doing all of the wonderful things I'd discovered I didn't just enjoy, but that I actually craved.

He sat up suddenly, his mouth coming down on my breast as his hands went to my waist. He worried at the flesh with his teeth and lips until I knew I'd be covered with marks. Then he took my nipple into his mouth and I swore.

"Cheater," I breathed as he sucked and bit until my nipple was swollen and throbbing. When he started on the other one, my stomach tightened and I knew I was close to coming. I was torn. On one hand, if I started riding him now, I'd come in seconds, but that meant I'd be giving in. My stubbornness won out.

He looked up at me, my nipple caught between his teeth. He pulled his head back, stretching my flesh until I cried out. My hands were trapped between us, folded against our stomachs.

"Are you in charge?" he asked his question again.

I started to nod, but everything disappeared in a wail when he did two things at once. The hands on my waist pushed me down as his hips snapped up, impaling me in one almost-brutal thrust that instantly made me come.

My head fell back as he held me against him, using his position to continue moving both of us. Each time I came down, I was met with his hips coming up, driving him deep. He gave me no respite, forcing one orgasm into another until I couldn't tell where one ended and the other began, and still he kept going. My arms and legs were limp, unable to process any commands I gave them – if I could've formed a coherent thought. At the moment, I was reduced to sounds of pleasure mixed with the occasional word or phrase.

"Yes! Please. Please. DeVon, yes."

Then he was biting down on the side of my throat and a new explosion went through me. I felt him coming inside me even as everything started to go gray. As consciousness began to fall away, I heard him say my name and I tucked my body against his, trusting him to take care of me. And then I let myself slip under.

# THREE

## DEVON

I looked down at the beautiful woman curled up against me and wondered, not for the first time, how I'd gotten so lucky.

I'd always considered myself the poster boy for the American dream. I'd come over from Italy when I was just eighteen with barely twenty dollars to my name and a scholarship to Berkley. Now, fifteen years later, I was the CEO of one of the biggest talent agencies in Hollywood and had more money than I knew what to do with. I'd paid my dues, worked my ass off. I'd had my heart broken and my trust betrayed, but I'd told myself that it had been good for me because it had made me see how people really were.

I'd slept with hundreds of women, indulging in fantasies most men could never hope to make real. Threesomes. Foursomes. Kinks that had run from a little bondage to out-and-out S&M. I'd never had relationships, only women I'd fucked. I'd never kept one around longer than a few weeks, not as a steady 'partner.' There'd been a couple that most people would've called fuck buddies, women who I'd been able to call any time, but who hadn't had any expectations. Whenever a woman had started to think she meant something to me other than a good fuck, it had been time to say good-bye.

Everything about my life, from the outside, had looked perfect. Hell, even I had thought it had been perfect. And then Krissy Jensen had walked into Mirage for a job interview. She'd been like no one I'd ever met before. Everything I'd thrown at her, she hadn't brushed off. She'd fought back. She hadn't cared who I was or how much money I had. Very few men had ever gone toe-to-toe with me. Krissy was the only woman who'd ever held her own with me. I had a feeling her friend Carrie might've been able to get close, maybe those other two women Krissy was friends with, but I doubted it. Krissy was the strongest person I knew, male or female, and it was one of the things I loved the most about her.

People who knew my sexual proclivities might've assumed that I'd want some submissive little mouse, the kind of woman who'd say, "Yes, Master," and take everything I gave her. Before, I'd liked that, but back then, sex hadn't meant the same. It had been about power and control. I'd always pleased my partners, never did anything they didn't just agree to but that they enjoyed. But it hadn't been about me wanting them to be happy. It had been selfish, me stroking my pride at how good a lover I was. It had taken me a long time, but I'd finally come to grips with the fact that because of what had happened between my ex-fiancée and my former best friend, I had the need to prove that she hadn't chosen him because I was bad in bed.

I brushed a few strands of silky hair back from Krissy's face, letting my fingers linger on her forehead before sliding down her cheek. A surge of love went through me. Admitting how I felt about her hadn't been easy. It had taken me months to actually say the words, "I love you," but she'd known that when I'd said them, they had been the truth, not something to say because it had been expected.

I'd always laughed at people when they'd talked about meeting their other half, or their soul mate. Even when I'd been with Haley and had thought that had been love, I hadn't believed in any of that shit. Meeting Krissy had turned everything upside down. She wasn't just my other half. She was what I'd have been if I'd been a woman. Smart. Strong. Fiery. She'd defied the expectations of her socialite mother and made her own way. Moved to New York City and then out to Los Angeles because she wanted to make something of herself. Not to prove anything to anyone, but because that had been what she'd wanted.

She was ambitious, but not ruthless in a typical Hollywood way. She'd do what needed to be done, but only if it didn't hurt the people she cared about. She worked hard, but money wasn't everything to her. She was compassionate to those who deserved it and brutal towards those who hurt the innocent.

I'd once seen her decimate a director who'd fired and then assaulted a thirteen-year-old client of ours because the boy had refused to have sex with him. There hadn't been enough evidence for official charges, but Krissy had taken it on anyway. I'd seen a lot of careers hit rock bottom and then rise to the top again. It wouldn't happen with Rudolph Delfire. He wasn't just through in Hollywood. Pretty much anyone with an internet connection knew what he'd been accused of and the kind of public humiliation they'd be subject to if they defended him.

I'd never seen anyone so driven. Except me, of course. She was everything I'd never known I wanted.

She was damn near perfect.

I kissed the top of her head and looked out the window at the clear blue skies. I knew she loved her adopted hometown of New York, especially since that's where her friends were, but I'd always prefer the West Coast. It was the beginning of July and the city had been brutally hot, but overcast half the time. At least if it was hot in LA, the sun would be out. Granted, there was always the smog to take into account, but we only had to deal with that when we were at the apartment in the city itself. Our house didn't get much smog.

Our house. Our apartment. Even though we'd been living together for a couple months, I was still getting used to the idea. Surprisingly, not in a bad way. After Haley, I'd never thought I'd ever want to live with someone. That was too much of a commitment, too much of a risk of being hurt. Krissy'd originally signed a six-month lease when she'd moved to LA and when she'd mentioned that she was debating looking for a nicer place when her lease was up, asking her to move in with me had just felt like the right thing to do. I'd been more nervous than I'd admitted, but it hadn't taken me long to realize that I loved living with her. That I didn't ever want her to not be there. Sure, she wasn't exactly the neatest person in the world, but she made the places looked lived in. Besides, I paid the cleaning crew well.

As it had been more frequently over the last few months, my gaze was drawn to Krissy's hand. Her left hand. My heart started to pound. I never wanted to lose Krissy and I never wanted to be with anyone else, but I wasn't sure where I stood on marriage. I'd proposed to Haley and, two days later, had caught her fucking my best friend. I knew Krissy would never do anything like that, but it was hard to shake the anxiety that came whenever I thought of making what I felt official. Fortunately, Krissy seemed content with where we were.

"Attention, passengers. This is your captain speaking. We'll be making our approach to LAX shortly."

I sighed. I hated to wake her, but we'd be landing soon. She hadn't gotten much sleep last night and it hadn't been my fault. We'd spent the Fourth of July with her friends, and then she and the other three women had decided they wanted to spend the entire night talking. Well, I wasn't sure if it was a conscious decision or not, but that's what had ended up happening, and Krissy had fallen asleep almost immediately after we'd boarded our flight back home.

"Krissy," I said softly. I gave her a little shake. "Babe, we're back."

She made a frustrated sound that brought a smile to my face. Even waking up, her hair a mess, her eyes full of sleep, she was beautiful. I kissed her forehead and handed her a bottle of water.

"I figured you would want a chance to wake up a bit before we landed."

She gave me a sleepy smile and rubbed her eyes.

I had the sudden urge to make a joke about Sleeping Beauty, but I knew Krissy. She'd most likely flip me off for the comment. My smile widened. We may not have been some Disney Princess and Prince Charming, but I would take our story over a fairy tale any day. We were making our own happy ending.

We made small talk as the two of us waited for our flight to land and then there was the usual hustle and bustle to get bags and catch taxis, though we were lucky enough not to have to deal with the latter. One of the benefits of having money meant we had a town car waiting for us. The driver was one we'd had before and he gave us both a smile as he opened the back door for us.

Once we were settled, I pulled out my phone and switched it off of airplane mode. It buzzed as a missed call came through, followed by a voicemail. I recognized the number even without the Caller ID. It was the agency. An extension didn't show, but since they'd left a message, I assumed it was important. Well, there was that and the fact that I'd given everyone the day off even though it was Monday. People in our line of work tended to spend quite a bit of time drinking on certain holidays, the Fourth being one of them. I had a feeling there were a lot my employees nursing hangovers today.

The message was brief, but I instantly recognized Melissa's voice. That made sense. My assistant would've gone in today, at least for a couple hours, even though I'd told her to take the day off, too. The only days she ever listened to me about were Christmas and Thanksgiving. Today, I was glad she hadn't stayed away.

I frowned as I hung up.

"What's wrong?" Krissy's voice was concerned.

"We have to head into the office," I said. I looked down at her. "Melissa called. Something's happened."

# FOUR
## KRISSY

I sighed as DeVon leaned up to knock on the window and tell the driver we were changing direction. I knew that for Melissa to have called DeVon, knowing we were just getting home, it had to be something big. I was just so tired. I'd been up late last night with my friends, but it wasn't like I hadn't pulled an all-nighter before. I really hoped I wasn't catching something. Summer colds were the worst.

When we arrived at the agency, Melissa was still there, looking decidedly put-out. It had to be why we were here rather than who was here with her. Everyone liked Landon.

Landon Sully was my age and absolutely gorgeous. With his thick, dark brown hair and piercing blue eyes, he was Mirage's top star. He'd gotten a big part in a movie a couple months ago and when it had been released last month, he'd become Holly-wood's 'it' boy. He was more than just a client, however. He was one of DeVon's few friends and one of the only ones I had on this coast. In fact, he'd been the one to tell both DeVon and me to stop being stupid and admit to what we felt for each other. Since that trip to Vegas, he'd been one of the few people that we'd spent much time with outside of professional functions.

Usually, he was outgoing, friendly and the life of the party. Today, however, his expression was more somber than I'd ever seen it. As we walked into DeVon's office, Melissa patted Landon on the shoulder and stood.

"If you need me," she said to DeVon. "Please call me in."

He nodded. "We'll take it from here."

We waited for Melissa to close the door behind her and then DeVon and I sat on either side of Landon.

"All right," DeVon said. His voice was business-like, but I could tell he was just as worried by Landon's unusual behavior as I was. "What's going on?"

Landon ran his hand through his hair. "I got a call from Garrison Mayflower."

Shit.

Whatever was going to follow this sentence couldn't be good. Garrison Mayflower was a name everyone in the entertainment industry knew, but not for any good reason. Mayflower was paparazzi. He didn't deserve to be called a reporter. His stories were nothing but pure sensationalism, whatever shit he could stir up.

And I had a bad feeling I knew what he'd found on Landon. And, unfortunately, it might not be false.

"I met with Jarrett Carr a few days ago," Landon began. "We were careful, but obviously not careful enough."

DeVon scowled.

It wasn't any surprise to DeVon or me that the up-and-coming action star was meeting with out comedy actor Jarrett Carr. We'd already known Landon was gay. DeVon, of course, had known it since moment one. I'd figured it out a few minutes after Landon and I had first met. His comments about checking out the hot MMA fighters hadn't exactly been subtle. Last year, he hadn't been public about his sexuality, but he hadn't hidden it, either. The difference between then and now, however, was that when we'd been hanging out in Vegas, Landon had been recognizable by some, but not the kind of person who drew crowds wherever he went. Since his movie's release, however, he'd become a household name.

The two of us and Landon had sat down once it had become clear the movie was going to be huge. We'd asked him what he wanted to do. At the time, he'd been photographed in groups, flirting with different women, but never anything that could specifically say which team he played for. We all knew how this worked. A comedian could be gay without a problem. It was okay to be funny and like the same gender. Someone with theater roots who played the sensitive best friends in romantic dramas or comedies could also come out without having an issue. Older men who had a history of dignified roles were also okay.

A gay action star was a different story.

We'd laid the facts out for Landon and told him that Mirage would support whatever decision he made. He'd decided on a compromise. If anyone asked him directly, he wouldn't deny it. However, he wouldn't officially come out, either. He wasn't in a relationship and had no problem keeping his dating discreet, so we'd agreed that we wouldn't hide it, but we wouldn't advertise it, either.

"Okay," DeVon said. "Mayflower has pictures of you and Carr. What else is there, Landon?"

DeVon was right. If it had just been Landon and Jarrett having a meal or walking around together, there wouldn't have been a story. Mayflower would've put the pictures online or sent them to TMZ for speculation, but no one would've cared. Every other day, people were posting pictures of Landon having lunch with some supermodel or actress. He was a friendly guy and the fact that he was seen with different women all the time only helped enhance a ladies' man reputation, something Mirage didn't encourage or discourage.

"Jarrett came by and we ordered some pizza," Landon said. "I didn't think anything of it because we were in the house. The curtains were closed and there's a gate that keeps people away."

I could picture the house in my head. Even though Landon was now a bankable star, he hadn't gone crazy with that first paycheck and bought some massive, million-dollar mansion. What he had done was get into a nice place in a gated community. Mirage had checked it out and their security was good. I couldn't figure out how anyone had gotten pictures of Jarrett and Landon that were compromising at all.

"Did the pizza guy take the photos?" DeVon asked.

My lawyer wheels started turning, thinking of the legal action we could take against the person who'd taken the pictures as well as the pizza place.

"No." Landon frowned. "I went to get the pizza and I was just wearing a pair of shorts."

I had a feeling I knew where this was going.

"Jarrett was wearing a little less when he came up behind me and wrapped his arms around me right before the door closed." Landon's cheeks flushed.

"Shit," DeVon breathed. "And that's what Mayflower got a picture of?"

"That and pretty much everything Jarrett has to offer."

"Well, Jarrett's already out, so at least we don't have to work with his people on this one," I said. "That means it's pretty much your choice as to how we handle this."

"Mayflower said we'll have to pay a million dollars to keep the pictures out of the press," Landon said. He gave me a pleading look. "I'm not ashamed of who I am, Krissy, but I can't come out like this. Whoever Mayflower gets those pictures to will spin some sort of sleazy story. I'll be a joke. You know I don't take myself that seriously, but this is different. Jarrett's a nice guy and I don't want him getting caught up in this."

I reached over and took Landon's hand between both of mine. DeVon put his hand on his friend's shoulder.

"You can't pay him," Landon said, turning to look at DeVon.

DeVon shook his head. "I'm not going to, but I am going to kick his ass."

I rolled my eyes, but there was only affection in my voice. "We're not going to pay because I'm going to take care of it."

"Really?" The hopeful expression on Landon's face made him look much younger than he was.

"Hey, I'm a badass lawyer, remember?" I smiled at him. "I handled divorces in New York. I think I can deal with one slimy LA paparazzi."

"Thank you," Landon said, relief evident in his voice.

I was still smiling, but inside I was seething. I despised the paparazzi. It was one thing if people were out in public, but even then it was iffy. To spy on someone at home...that just pissed me off. And then to try and blackmail such a nice guy as Landon just because people couldn't handle him being a gay action star...Oh, I'd handle Mayflower, all right. And he'd be lucky if I didn't ruin his already shitty career while I was at it.

"Are you going to be okay?" DeVon asked. "You want to come over for a drink?"

"No." Landon shook his head. He suddenly looked as tired as I felt. "I just want to go home."

"You do that and leave Mayflower to me," I said. "I'll keep you posted on how things go."

Landon nodded and stood. DeVon and I did the same. We watched our friend leave. When the door closed, I sighed.

"This sucks," I said.

"It does," DeVon agreed. "I wish people would just stop

being assholes about people's personal lives. Like who he loves changes whether or not he's good at his job."

I wrapped my arms around his waist and squeezed. "Have I told you lately just how much I love you?"

He put his arms around me and hugged me back. "Yes, but I always like to hear it." He kissed the top of my head. "Now, let's go home."

# FIVE

## DEVON

This situation with Landon was bothering Krissy more than she let on. I hated it, too. Landon was a client I also considered a friend. In the months since Krissy and I had started dating, the three of us had become even closer. I knew she hadn't been happy that I'd agreed to help Landon keep things quiet, but she hadn't said anything. We agreed that it was Landon's choice, but we both hated that it was something that even had to be considered.

Krissy was quiet on the ride back to the house and I knew she was thinking about how she was going to deal with things. I still wanted to handle Mayflower my way, but mostly because I was itching to punch the bastard's smug face. She was definitely more qualified to handle things like this simply because she had been a lawyer. Granted, that was divorce and not entertainment, but she thought like a lawyer either way.

I reached over and took her hand as we walked into the house. It was funny, I thought, how just her living here made this place feel more like home than just a house. I'd hired a decorator for both the apartment and the house when I'd first bought them and she'd done a great job, but it had never really felt like me. Gradually, Krissy had been changing things so that every place looked lived in. Before, the only part of the entire house that I'd given a personal touch was my bedroom and that was because that had been the only place where it was only ever me.

Until Krissy.

There wasn't much I could say she was my first or only for, but there were two. She was the only woman who'd ever slept in my bedroom. In what was now our bedroom. Any women who'd slept over in the past had done so in a guest room. Without me. After we'd finish, I'd always retired to my room and leave the women a note and cab fare. The drawers that had once held envelopes of money and notes were empty. The guest room was just a guest room.

The only other thing that was exclusively hers was what I suddenly needed to feel. Me inside her, nothing between us. Skin against skin. Delicious friction and heat until I exploded inside her, filling her. She was the only person I'd ever had that with. The only person I'd ever trusted enough.

"Come on." I pulled her towards our room. "Let's finish our vacation on a good note. We can worry about the whole Landon thing tomorrow. There's nothing we're going to do now anyway."

She still looked tired as we walked down the hallway, but the gleam in her eyes said she wanted me as much as I wanted her. That wasn't surprising. We seemed to always want each other. Tonight, I was going to do something we didn't do very often. No kink, no rough stuff. Just me making slow, sweet love to her until we both came and then fell asleep in each other's arms.

When we stepped into the bedroom, I wrapped my arms around her and pulled her back against me. I nuzzled the side of her neck, breathing deep the scent of her floral body wash and of her. My cock stirred. Just being close to her, smelling her, it was enough to make me hard. I pressed my lips against the hollow just under her ear.

"I want you," I whispered.

"I want you, too." She pressed back against me a little more firmly and then reached for the bottom of her shirt.

I put my hands over hers. "Let me take care of you."

She nodded as her hands dropped to her sides. I felt her entire body relax against me and a surge of love and protectiveness went through me. I still had a hard time believing just how much I loved this woman.

I took the hem of her shirt in my hands. "Lift your arms."

She did and I slowly peeled her shirt off of her. I kissed her spine at the base of her neck and then undid the braid she'd been wearing for our trip. I massaged her scalp as I ran my fingers through her thick, dark hair. I loved her hair. Loved seeing it spread out on a pillow while I was stretched out above her. The feel of it on my thighs when she was going down on me. The weight of it in my hand when I took her from behind.

"Mmm." She moaned as I worked my way down her neck to her shoulders. "That feels good."

I slid my hands down her arms and laced my fingers between hers. I pressed my lips to her shoulder, then over the dark mark I'd made on her neck the other night. My chest tightened. I loved that she let me do that, loved that she did the same to me. I released her hands and slid mine up her stomach to cup her breasts. She was wearing plain cotton, chosen more for comfort during our trip than for sex appeal, but it didn't matter. She was sexy no matter what she was wearing.

The thing I liked the best about this particular bra, however, wasn't the cut or fabric. It was the fact that it had a front clasp, which made undressing her from behind all the more appealing. My fingers made short work of the hooks, years of experience allowing me to manage all but the trickiest of women's garments with little thought. My hands caressed the soft skin as it was exposed and I used my teeth to pull first one strap, then the other, off her shoulders.

She took in a shuddering breath as my fingers gently rubbed over her hardening nipples. I'd been rough with them during our vacation and I knew they were sore. Sometimes, that meant I'd be just as rough, drawing out gasps of painful pleasure as I pulled on them, but not tonight.

My hands dropped to her waist, quickly undoing the button and zipper to her jeans. I didn't take them off, though, not quite yet. I wrapped one arm high around her waist, my hand covering one breast. The other hand, I slid beneath the waistband of her pants and then beneath her white cotton panties.

"DeVon." She moaned my name as my fingers slipped between her folds.

My cock hardened. Damn. I loved hearing her say my name like that. It was as good as when she screamed it.

I rubbed my fingers on either side of her clit, putting just the right amount of pressure on that little bundle of nerves. A shiver ran the full length of her body. I began to make small circles across the top of her clit, smiling as Krissy's body began to jerk against mine.

"I love how you respond to me," I murmured. I sucked her earlobe into my mouth, nibbling on it as I continued my ministrations to her clit. It didn't take long for her to make the breathless little sounds that I knew meant she was close to coming. "I've got you," I whispered in her ear as she let herself go.

Her body stiffened and I could feel the tips of my fingers getting wet as she soaked her panties. She made a frustrated noise as I pulled my hand out of her pants. I reached up and brushed a finger across her lips. Her mouth opened automatically and I slid my fingers inside. My eyes closed as she began to suck her juices from my fingers, each pull going straight south.

Her tongue swirled around the digits in her mouth and my cock pressed painfully against my zipper.

I took a step back, removing my fingers from her mouth and dropping my hands to her waist. I took her panties down with her jeans and helped her balance as she stepped out of them. When she was completely naked, I motioned for her to lie on the bed. She slid backwards across the comforter and leaned against the pillows. Her fingers twitched and I knew she wanted to touch herself, but she wouldn't do it, not unless I gave her permission. I smiled at her and removed my clothes, dropping them on the floor with hers.

Without a word, I crawled up the bed, loving the way she watched me, how her gaze caressed every inch of my body. She licked her lips and I groaned. I'd gotten head from a lot of women, but no one else's mouth had felt like hers. Soft velvet heat. Wet, flexible tongue. I was too big around for most women to take all the way to the base, but she did it, sometimes holding herself there until I lost control and spilled down her throat. She was the only woman who'd ever been able to make me lose control.

I spread her legs and stretched out between them. I always made sure she came at least twice, even if I spent hours edging her, making her wait and beg for relief. I wasn't going to do that tonight. Neither was I going to torture her with multiple orgasms, forcing her to climax over and over until she pleaded with me to stop. As much as I enjoyed doing both of those things, tonight I was keeping it simple.

I lowered my head and ran my tongue along the sensitive skin that glistened with evidence of her release. She moaned, her hands brushing through my hair as I began to make love to her with my mouth. I dipped my tongue inside her before moving up to her clit. I wrapped my lips around it, sucking gently while flicking the tip of my tongue across it. She tugged on my hair, sending signals that should've been pain but were more pleasure racing from my scalp.

My cock throbbed, begging me to bury myself inside her, to thrust into her tight, wet heat until I exploded. I ignored it. She came first.

Her hips bucked up against my mouth but I kept the slow, steady rhythm. Long, broad strokes with the flat of my tongue. Deep explorations. Firm pressure on her clit. And then she was coming, crying out my name and pushing my face harder against her. I let her ride out her orgasm, coaxing every last drop of pleasure from her until her hands fell away.

I crawled up her body, our bodies barely touching until I settled between her legs. I propped myself up on my elbows so that my full weight wasn't on her. She looked up at me and wrapped her legs around my waist so that her heels rested on the backs of my knees. Our eyes met and I surged forward. Her mouth opened in a silent cry, her pussy spasming around my cock as I filled her. She was still my perfect fit. Tight enough that the sensation of entering her that first time was always intense, but not so much so that it was a fight to get inside her. I gave her a moment, and then began to move.

My strokes were deep, but slow, and I didn't rush, didn't pound into her until she was writhing beneath me. As our bodies moved together, I lowered my head until my mouth covered hers. My tongue pushed between her lips, mimicking the movements below. Her tongue curled around mine even as she wrapped her arms around me, pulling me down against her.

Our bodies were flush together as I thrust into her, rubbing against her clit with every stroke. Her nails dug into my back and I felt her body begin to shake. I broke the kiss, wanting to see her face when she came. Her eyes were dark and wild, a brown that was almost black. Her skin was flushed, her lips swollen from my kiss. They parted and she cried out, her back arching as she came. Her pussy squeezed my cock almost painfully and I pressed my face against the side of her throat, calling out her name as pleasure rushed through me. My hips jerked against her as my cock pulsed and emptied deep inside her.

We lay there for a moment, our breath hot and heavy against each other's skin. I could feel her heart pounding in her chest, the rhythm complementing my own. We both shuddered as I slid out of her, and I had to take a moment before I could get to my feet. I headed into the bathroom to clean up and returned with a damp cloth. She was already half-asleep as I gently wiped her off. When I finished, I tossed the washcloth into the hamper and then slid Krissy under the sheets before climbing under myself. I pulled her close, her back against my chest, and she was asleep before we'd even fully settled.

I kissed her temple and tightened my hold. I'd never imagined that my life could be so perfect.

# SIX

## DEVON

I woke up about a half an hour before my alarm would've gone off and it took me a minute to realize why. Krissy wasn't in bed next to me. She was in the bathroom and I could hear her getting sick.

Concern broke through the fog of sleep surrounding me and I climbed out of bed.

"Babe," I called softly as I headed for the bathroom. "You okay?" I always thought that was a stupid question to ask someone who was obviously throwing up, but I couldn't really think of anything else to ask.

"Yeah."

I winced at the reply. Krissy was the kind of person who hated to show weakness, even when sick, so she'd never admit how bad she felt, but I could hear it in her voice. Still, I knew she wouldn't want me just barging in, and she'd be honest if she needed my help or not. Yet another of the ways the two of us worked well together.

"Do you want me to come in?"

"No," she sighed. "Not really anything you can do."

"Do you want me to call off and stay home with you?"

"No."

The toilet flushed and then I heard running water. I waited. A couple minutes later, the door opened. She was pale, her hair a mess from sleep, but she was still the most beautiful woman I'd ever seen. She pulled on her robe and gave me a weak smile.

"I think it was a combination of airplane food and jet lag," she said. "Just give me a couple hours of sleep and I'll be good to go."

I kissed her forehead, but didn't try to help her into bed. I'd learned last December not to do that unless she asked. She hated being coddled when she was sick.

I glanced at the clock as she settled back against the pillows with another sigh. "I'm going to go ahead in early if you don't want me to stay."

"That's fine," she said. Her eyes were already closed. "I might be a little late."

"Get some rest," I said. "Call me if you're not coming in so I don't worry."

She nodded. "Love you."

I smiled even though she couldn't see it. "I love you, too. Feel better."

I didn't wait for a response because I knew she was already asleep. I headed into the bathroom to shower. She was still sleeping when I came out and I checked on her again before I left. I really hoped this was exactly what she said it was. I hated seeing her sick even more than I hated being sick myself. And it wasn't just because I didn't want her to be miserable.

Part of me, no matter how much I tried to hide it, was still the scared teenager who'd watched his mother waste away for nearly two years before she'd finally passed. I'd had to be strong then, for my father, for my little brother. I'd been eleven when she'd first gotten sick. Franco had only been five. After more than twenty years, I still missed her, but enough time had passed that the memories were more wistful and pleasant than sad. Still, when Krissy got sick, I couldn't stop myself from remembering the falsely bright smile on my mother's face when she'd told me she was ill, but that she'd get better soon. That had been the first time I'd realized that parents lied.

The logical part of me said that I was over-reacting, so I listened to it and reminded myself of it repeatedly as I headed into the agency. Usually, when I came into Mirage after some time away, I felt a surge of pride when I saw the steel and glass building that housed the talent agency I'd spent the last five years building. Today, however, I was too distracted to do anything more than greet my employees as I passed.

I'd gotten there early enough that my agents weren't there yet, but Melissa was. Sometimes, I wondered if she ever actually went home. She frowned as she saw me, but didn't ask what was wrong. Other than Krissy, Melissa was probably the person who knew me best. Considering she'd actually been my assistant since before I'd started Mirage, that wasn't really a surprise. She'd been the only one who'd come with me when I'd gone out on my own.

I gave her a tight smile. "Krissy might not be in today. She's not feeling well."

Melissa nodded. "Do you want me to cancel any appointments later today so you can leave early?"

"Not yet," I said. "She thinks it was just jet lag."

"Your first appointment is right after lunch," she continued as she followed me into my office. "Steven Morrison wants to talk about re-casting a role for a series that was just green-lit."

"Thanks, Melissa." I sighed as I saw the stack of papers on my desk. I knew I'd have at least twice as many emails. Krissy and I had promised each other that we wouldn't even check our email while on vacation. I was beginning to regret that decision.

At least I could look forward to meeting with Steven. He was one of the few directors I actually liked. Plus, this project could be huge. Landon's movie was doing well enough that he was becoming a household name. I had half a dozen movie offers for him, but I was leaning towards Steven's re-casting. This series promised to be the next big thing and Steven's lead was proving to be a real pain in the ass. The plan was to kill off his character in the second episode and introduce another character who would be taking over. I was going to pitch Landon for the role.

I frowned as I sat down. After this whole paparazzi thing, maybe it wasn't such a good idea. I knew Steven wouldn't care that Landon was gay, but if this hit the fan when Steven was trying to convince the studio to go along with the casting, it might complicate things. Hollywood tried to project a tolerant, accepting community, but some of the big-wigs were still bigoted assholes when it came to homosexuality. Then again, Krissy said she was going to handle things so there was a good possibility that nothing would come of it anyway. At least, that's what I was hoping.

I turned on my computer and started on the paperwork while I waited for things to boot up. I put the whole Landon thing out of my head and focused on the work. Most of it was routine and I found myself falling back into the rhythm of the work. A lot of people in Hollywood thought all I did was play, but I actually did as much work as the rest of my staff. Some of that work included going to parties and premieres, but it was still work.

I'd been at it for more than two hours when Melissa buzzed me.

"Yes?" I glanced at the phone, wondering if Krissy had an

issue calling my personal line. We'd been having some problems with our phones. We were scheduled for a repair in two days.

"You have a visitor."

I waited for some sort of explanation or a name, but nothing came. That was strange. I'd never known Melissa to be so abrupt, but I supposed she had a good reason.

"All right," I replied. "Send them in."

A dozen possibilities ran through my mind. Some reporter who didn't want me to know who he was. Some high-up executive who had an issue with something I'd done. Maybe it was Mayflower and Melissa was so annoyed by him that she'd gotten distracted. Or, better yet, maybe it was Krissy coming in to surprise me. We generally tried to keep our physical relationship out of the office, but every so often, we gave in to the temptation and had a little fling.

When the door opened, a woman walked in. She had wavy black hair that fell just past her shoulders. Hazel eyes that were fixed on me from the moment she entered the office. She was about average height, a little too curvy to be slender. In some ways, she actually resembled Krissy.

But she was definitely not Krissy.

It had been almost seven years since I'd last seen Sasha Richmond, but I recognized her immediately. Now I knew why Melissa hadn't said anything. She'd been my assistant back when Sasha and I had been 'dating' and knew things hadn't ended well. Sasha had been in her early twenties when we'd met and she'd been exactly my type. An insatiable sexual appetite and a willingness to submit had been the most important qualities I'd looked for at the time. I'd thought I'd made things clear to her when I'd first approached her, that this wouldn't be a relationship, she wouldn't be my girlfriend. I'd told her that it was fucking, pure and simple, a pursuit of physical pleasure. She'd agreed, but I hadn't realized until a couple days into it that she hadn't truly accepted what I'd said.

When I'd first broken things off with her, she'd cried and begged, which weren't things I hadn't seen before. Once those things had failed to move me, she'd moved on to threats and insults. Again, not uncommon. A week after I'd dumped her, however, she'd progressed to following me around, showing up at work and home. I'd tried ignoring her. I'd tried politely explaining things again. Finally, after more than a month, I'd been forced to take out a restraining order. I'd called the police on her twice for violating it, and she'd disappeared.

Until now.

"Sasha." I kept my voice even. I didn't think the restraining order was still effective since I hadn't bothered to check into it once she'd stopped bothering me. I had security guards who'd escort her out if I needed it, but I decided to wait and see what she wanted. The last thing I wanted was her to make a scene.

"Hi, DeVon." The smile she gave me was surprisingly sane.

"It's been a while." I gestured for her to sit.

She nodded and took a seat. "Thank you for seeing me."

I didn't say anything, waiting for her to share why she'd come. I didn't have to wait long.

"First, I wanted to say that I'm sorry about how things turned out."

That was progress, but I was still wary. "Thank you," I said. "Apology accepted."

She looked down, picking at her dress slacks. With a start, I realized that she was nervous.

I sighed. I appreciated that she came to apologize, but I really didn't have the time or the patience to deal with Sasha's drama right now. "What's going on, Sasha?"

She gave a little laugh and raised her head. "I see the years haven't taught you to soften your tongue." Her eyes gleamed. "Which isn't a bad thing if that tongue's buried in my cunt."

I resisted the urge to tell her to get out and instead just asked, "Why are you here?"

She smiled a devious smile. "I'm here to tell you about your son."

# SEVEN

# KRISSY

I felt like shit.

I groaned as I rolled onto my back, the motion making my stomach roil. I'd woken up early, knowing I was going to throw up, and I'd run into the bathroom. At the time, I'd been sure that it had been a combination of airplane food and jet lag. It didn't usually bother me, but since DeVon wasn't sick and we'd eaten the same thing, I'd known it hadn't been food poisoning. I supposed I could be coming down with the flu, but I didn't want to consider that. With this whole Landon thing going on, I couldn't afford to get sick, even with a twenty-four hour bug.

I'd told DeVon that I'd just needed some sleep, but when I woke up in the middle of the morning and still had a pounding headache and a queasy stomach, I wasn't so sure. I laid there for a few minutes, waiting to see if things would settle down, but every little movement I made just made matters worse.

I swore, but quietly because even my own voice would be too loud for the pain in my head. If it had just been the headache or a cold, I would've drugged myself up and gone in anyway. I'd done it before, despite DeVon's protests. A stomach flu, however, was a different story. If I couldn't even get out of bed without throwing up, how was I supposed to get dressed, survive the entire ride to the office and then take an elevator to get to my office? And that was only getting to work. After that, I'd actually have to do stuff. I was exhausted just thinking about it.

I groaned and closed my eyes. I hated to do it, but I was going to have to call off. I reached over to the end table for my phone. I needed to let DeVon know, both so he didn't worry, but also because he needed to decide if the whole Landon thing could wait until tomorrow or if he wanted to take care of it himself. I wasn't sure it'd be such a good idea for him to do that, but better him than Mirage's legal counsel. Leon Duncan was a great lawyer, but he was better at making things go away by smoothing things over. I didn't want things smoothed over with Mayflower. The reporter was a bastard and I wanted to tear him a new one.

I called DeVon's personal work line first, but there was no answer. I glanced at the time. He shouldn't have been out to lunch, but I supposed he could've been on another call. We had been gone for several days. I had no doubt that there were massive amounts of work to do.

I felt a stab of guilt. I was supposed to be DeVon's assistant, training to be a full partner. Essentially, I was his partner, not just in our personal lives. I should be there working with him.

I knew what he'd say, though. He'd tell me to take care of myself. Actually, he'd probably tell me to go to the hospital, have dozens of tests run to find out exactly what was wrong with me. Now I was thinking it might have been a good thing that I hadn't gotten ahold of DeVon. He did tend to over-react when it came to my health. I understood, though. I hadn't gotten the whole story because I hadn't wanted to pry, but I knew that his mother died when he'd been a kid and it had been some sort of long-term illness.

I called his cell, knowing he kept it on vibrate but checked every hour or so in case any important calls came in. His dad's health was better than it had been a year ago, but he was still fairly weak. DeVon always made himself reachable.

My call did go to voicemail, but that wasn't unusual. "Hey, babe, it's me. I'm still feeling pretty bad and I'm not going to come in today. I'm going to call Mayflower and set up a meet for tomorrow, so that should keep things calm today. I'm going to try to sleep this thing away, so don't worry about trying to call me back. Have a good day and I'll see you when you get home. Love you."

I ended the call and then went into my contacts folder. I didn't put Mayflower on the same level of the other reporters I usually interacted with, but I had his contact number anyway. Mirage had unfortunately dealt with him in the past, so his had been a number given to me when I'd started at the agency.

I dialed the number and then breathed a sigh of relief when Mayflower didn't answer. I might've wanted to make sure this thing was done right, but I wasn't sure I could handle a phone confrontation with him right now. I'd rather leave a message and let that be the communication until we met face-to-face.

"Mr. Mayflower, this is Krissy Jensen from Mirage. I'd like to meet with you tomorrow to discuss the issue with Landon Sully." I gave him a time and the name of my favorite little restaurant. If I was going to have to meet with a jackass, I might as well have good food while I was doing it.

My stomach flipped.

If I could eat tomorrow, that was.

I ended the call, put the phone back on the table and then snuggled back down into my bed and hoped I'd fall asleep before I felt the need to vomit again. Fortunately, I did just that.

I woke once, mid-afternoon, and felt a bit better, though still not one hundred percent. The nausea had gone away, thankfully, but I still felt dizzy and weak. I managed to hold down some water and then went back to sleep.

When I woke up the next time, it was dark and I heard DeVon moving around in the room. I rolled over, blinking at the light coming from the bathroom.

"Sorry, Babe," DeVon said quietly. "I didn't mean to wake you."

"It's okay," I said sleepily. "What time is it?"

He looked at the bedside clock. "Almost six. How are you feeling?"

I paused a moment to consider the question. "Better," I said. "But still not great."

He nodded and it was then that I noticed the absent look on his face.

"Are you okay?" I asked.

"Fine." He un-tucked his shirt. "You want me to make you something to eat? Soup?"

"I don't think we have any," I said as I pushed myself up into a sitting position.

"I'll order some," he said.

I watched him walk out without another word. I frowned. I didn't expect him to fawn all over me when I was sick. In fact, I preferred that he didn't, but DeVon was always attentive when I was sick. And as affectionate as I'd let him be. Even when it was just cramps, he would always ask what I needed and then kiss my forehead before going to get it.

I sighed and closed my eyes. Soup sounded good, but sleep sounded even better. Maybe I'd take a little nap while I waited for it to be delivered. If I got enough sleep tonight, I'd be up to working tomorrow and maybe even remember to ask DeVon why he'd acted so strange tonight. If I didn't, it wasn't that important. He was here and that was what mattered.

# EIGHT
## KRISSY

I woke up when my alarm went off, but DeVon was already gone. That wasn't unusual. There were often times when he would get up early or not be able to sleep and would head into the office without waking me up.

My stomach was a bit sensitive, but I didn't feel like I was going to throw up if I stood, so that was better. I showered and dressed, feeling much more like myself by the time I headed into the kitchen to get myself something bland to eat and drink.

There was a note on the table. I read it quickly.

If you're in the kitchen, I'm hoping that means you're feeling better. If you're up to coming to work today, please contact Mayflower and deal with the Landon issue. If you don't think you can, call Melissa and she'll field it out. Don't push yourself. I don't want you getting sicker. I shouldn't be working late today. Love you. D

I frowned. There wasn't anything specifically wrong with the note, but something about it just seemed...absent, like he was writing it while his thoughts were elsewhere. That wasn't like him. He was usually hyper-focused. I shook my head. He was probably just distracted by all of the work we'd gotten behind on.

While I rummaged through the cabinets to find something to eat, I called DeVon's direct line. No answer. Again. I tried his cell and it went straight to voicemail. I frowned. Either he'd just rejected my call or his phone was off, neither of which was normal. I didn't dwell on it, though. My queasy stomach was demanding something.

"Got your note," I said as I pulled some crackers out. "I'm going to meet Mayflower this morning and then I'll be coming in. Talk to you then."

I nibbled on the crackers while I finished getting ready and then headed out to meet Mayflower. It was already hot when I stepped outside even though it wasn't even noon yet. I grimaced. I loved the LA sunshine, but I wasn't too fond of city heat.

Fortunately, Garrison Mayflower was early so we arrived within a few minutes of each other. He was a short, squat man with a pot belly and thinning, mousey brown hair. He looked like he hadn't shaved in two days and smelled like he hadn't bathed in longer than that. I wasn't a superficial person when it came to respecting or liking someone, but people who didn't bother with basic hygiene or even try with their appearance made it difficult for me to take them seriously. For Mayflower, the last straw was the trail of food stains down the front of his sweat-stained Hawaiian shirt.

"Let's not waste each other's time," I said as we sat in a shaded portion of the patio. "We both know why we're here. You're trying to blackmail my client and I'm here to tell you to go to hell."

He grinned, revealing teeth that looked like they hadn't seen the business end of a toothbrush since Clinton was president. "Blackmail is such an ugly word."

"But accurate." I folded my arms. "And illegal."

His smile widened.

"I'm going to keep this simple," I said. "If you try to pursue this matter, Mirage will be taking legal action against both you and whatever paper you try to sell those pictures to. We'll also be putting out the word that Mirage will cut all ties without anyone who publishes anything you write."

He rolled his eyes and my temper flared. I barely kept myself in check.

"You think if it were that simple, every agency or celebrity wouldn't try the same thing?" He picked something out of his teeth and flicked it away. "LA cops got a lot better things to do than worry about some pretty-boy fag getting outed."

It was all I could do not to reach across the table and knock out a couple of those rotting teeth. "If you think we're paying you, you're more of an idiot than you are a bigot."

He waved his hand in the air. "Pay, don't pay. I know quite a few papers and magazines that will pay good for pictures of Sully with his little fairy. And I got plenty to spread around."

"If you do this," I spoke through gritted teeth. "I will make it my personal mission to destroy you."

"You're a real firecracker, ain't you?" He looked me up and down.

I was going to need a shower after this meeting. I could feel the slime on my skin.

"Tell ya what," he said. "I'll cut you a discount. Half a million."

I wanted to tell him to shove his 'discount' up his ass, but I didn't. That wasn't beyond the realm of possibilities, but I had a bad feeling there was a catch. He didn't take long to reveal it.

"And you."

"Excuse me?" I snapped.

"Mirage pays me half a million and I get a night with you.

You get the pictures and a signed statement that I'll never reveal those pictures to anyone."

I opened my mouth to tell him to fuck himself, but snapped my jaw shut again. There had to be some way to use what he'd said against him. I stood. "We're done here."

"Suit yourself." He shrugged. "You've got until the end of the week or I go public." He reached down and grabbed his crotch. "You'll love what I got for you."

The thought of him touching me, of me touching him, made me feel sick. I hurried away without another word. I needed to get to Mirage and tell DeVon about the counter-offer. I swore under my breath as I thought about how my boyfriend was going to react to the proposition. Mayflower would be lucky if all he ended up with was a lawsuit.

I went straight up to his office. Melissa wasn't at her desk, so I just went straight in. When we'd first met, I'd made a habit of barging in, usually fuming about something or other. Now, I still rarely knocked but my mood was usually a better one.

"You're never going to believe what that bastard want..." My voice trailed off as I realized the office was empty. I looked towards the private bathroom, but the door was open. I frowned and looked at my watch. It wasn't lunchtime. Maybe he had a meeting. I turned and headed back out to wait for Melissa. She always knew where DeVon was. We joked that she was his work-wife and I knew she appreciated that I understood her relationship with DeVon. There was no jealousy there, only love and admiration.

"Krissy." She looked surprised to see me as she came out of the private administrator's bathroom. "How are you feeling?"

"Better," I said. I was still a little nauseous, but after what I'd just been told, that wasn't exactly surprising. "Is DeVon at a meeting?"

If I hadn't known Melissa so well, I wouldn't have noticed

the slight lift to her eyebrows or the surprise that flitted across her face. Her expression quickly settled into the polite mask of a professional.

"Melissa?" I tried to keep my voice even.

"DeVon hasn't been in yet," Melissa said. "And he's not expected in at all today."

"Where is he?" Concern and anger were warring inside me. He hadn't known for sure that I was coming in, so him scheduling off-site meetings without me wasn't anything to get worked up about.

Melissa's mouth tightened minutely. "I don't know where he is, Krissy. I'm sorry."

I walked towards the elevator, my head spinning. Where was DeVon? Why didn't Melissa know? And why hadn't he told me? What was he hiding?

# NINE

## DEVON

I hated lying to Krissy, even if it was more of a lie by omission than an actual lie. It wasn't that I wanted to hide anyone from her, more that I was still processing things myself, and until I knew what I thought about this entire situation, I didn't want to drag Krissy into it. The worst part of it was that I didn't know if I could wrap my head around everything without talking to Krissy about it. I'd spent my entire life making decisions on my own, important ones, but over the past year, I'd come to see just how much I relied on Krissy. Not in a bad way, but more as a sounding board and someone to keep me accountable. She was the only person I didn't feel like I needed to have complete control over, the only one who I let see me vulnerable.

I raked my hand through my hair as I got out of my car. As much as I prided myself on my strength and independence, my ability to take charge, I couldn't help but wish Krissy was walking with me into Kitchen 24. Having her next to me would've helped keep me steady. I'd never met a situation I couldn't handle, but this wasn't anything I'd ever considered happening. Before Krissy, I'd always used a condom and I'd always made sure to ask about birth control for extra protection.

Very few of the women I'd been with hadn't been on the pill, too. In fact, I was pretty sure I could count the number on one hand, including my ex-fiancée, Haley. Sasha hadn't been one of them.

She was waiting when I walked into the restaurant and I could tell by the look on her face that she wasn't happy with the location I'd picked. It wasn't exactly out of the way or hidden, but it wasn't the kind of restaurant that celebrities frequented either. I hadn't yet started Mirage when Sasha and I had been together, but I'd been talking about it and had already been a big deal at the agency where I'd worked before. I wondered that if, in Sasha's mind, I had been supposed to 'take her with me' when I made it even bigger. She'd always wanted to go parties and meet famous people. It had turned her on to be around the rich and famous, and I'd been willing to oblige considering how wild she'd gotten. It hadn't been until I'd ended things that I'd seen 'wild' hadn't been the right word to describe her. Obsessive, maybe even a bit psychotic.

I didn't want that crazy anywhere near Krissy. Not that I didn't think Krissy could handle herself. More that I didn't want her to need to. If it hadn't been for what Sasha had said, I would've told her to leave me alone and threatened her with an arrest if she came near me or Krissy. Things, however, weren't that simple.

I had a son.

Or, at least, that's what Sasha claimed.

I hadn't given her a chance to explain yesterday. I didn't want to risk anyone overhearing what we were talking about. I trusted Melissa more than anyone except Krissy, but most of my employees knew they could come talk to me at any time. The last thing I needed was some client or someone else barging in in the middle of Sasha's explanation. Kitchen 24 was a nice place, particularly for someone like me who wasn't exactly trying to hide, but wasn't advertising who I was. Chances of running into someone I knew were slim.

"DeVon." Sasha beamed at me as I approached the table. "I was beginning to think you'd picked this place so you could stand me up."

I ignored the comment and sat down across from where she was sitting. Things like this were typical of Sasha and one of the reasons we lasted about a week. The sex had been good enough that I might've kept her around for a bit longer, but she'd been crazy enough that it hadn't been worth it.

I quickly ordered when the waiter came by, keeping things simple. Sasha looked disappointed that I didn't want to linger, but rattled off her order as well. The most expensive things on the menu, of course. I didn't care. I could more than cover a meal. I was worried about what else she was going to try to weasel out of me and what the possibility was that I actually did have a kid.

"I suppose you want the story," she said with a sigh. "I had hoped we could make some small talk first, share what we've both been up to for the past six years."

"I want to know what happened and why you've waited six years to come to me." I took a sip of my water, proud that I'd managed to keep my voice even.

"Well," she said coyly. "One night, you stuck that huge cock of yours–"

"Knock it off, Sasha," I interrupted. "You know what I mean."

She nodded, a half-pout on her face, the kind that she liked to use when someone spoiled her fun. "About six weeks after we...parted ways, I found out I was pregnant."

"You told me you were on the pill," I said.

She ducked her head and peeked up through her lashes. "I lied. I'm sorry. I just wanted you so badly and I knew if I told you I wasn't on the pill, you wouldn't wait until I'd used it enough for it to be effective. I wasn't sure you'd want to fuck me without it."

With every moment that passed, I was regretting more that I'd fucked her in the first place.

"So you're telling me that, basically, we hit in that small percentage of condoms that failed to prevent pregnancy?" Something passed across her eyes that told me that wasn't the whole story. "Sasha, what aren't you telling me?" I felt my voice automatically go to that place it went when I was in Dom mode.

It still worked on her. I watched her body automatically shift into the posture of a Sub. Shoulders down, chin down, gaze lowered. A year ago, her response would've gotten me hard in seconds and I would've ordered her into the bathroom for a quickie. Now, I found the lack of push back to be a turn-off. It hadn't been until Krissy that I'd realized that's what I'd truly wanted, someone to make me work for domination.

"I may have...helped."

"Sasha!" I practically barked her name.

She cowed and I got the impression that she was trying to show me that she was still my Sub, even after all these years. "The last two times we had sex, I poked holes in the condoms you had with you."

My stomach twisted and I stared at her, sickened. How had I ever been with someone like her?

"I just didn't want you to leave me." Her voice was pleading.

I closed my eyes and inhaled slowly. I had to get the whole story before I left. If this was really my kid, I couldn't just abandon him because I was pissed at Sasha.

"And you weren't with anyone else?" I opened my eyes as I asked the question.

"No." She shook her head, eyes wide. "It had been two

weeks before I met you since I'd last had sex, and I hadn't done it again until two months after things ended between us."

I tried not to think about the fact that she'd fucked someone else while pregnant with my child. There was always the chance she was lying. It wasn't like she was the most stable of people.

"Why didn't you come to me as soon as you found out?" I asked.

"I was afraid you'd tell me to get rid of him and I couldn't do that. He was our baby."

That just proved how little she knew me. I'd never have tried to force a woman into doing something she didn't want to do. I would've taken care of her and the baby from the beginning, been as involved as she wanted. I might not have been looking to have a family – especially not then and especially not with her – but I'd never have shirked my responsibilities or made a child pay for something he had no control over.

"I tried making it on my own these past six years, but it hasn't been easy," she said. "Always scraping by. Working two jobs. And then, for the past year, Emmett has been asking about his father, wanting to know why his friends had daddies but he didn't."

I shifted in my seat. I was still trying to wrap my head around the idea of being a father.

"I realized that I wasn't being fair to Emmett by denying him the chance to meet you," she continued. "I'd just been trying to think of the right place and time to tell you. Then I got laid off at my main job and my hours were cut way back at the diner where I'd been working, too."

My eyes narrowed. Here it came, the pitch for money.

"I stayed away as long as I could," she said. "Trying to make the best of it. I picked up odd jobs, but it was barely enough to keep a roof over our heads and food on the table. Things started getting really bad this week and I knew I didn't have a choice. You'd never let your family starve."

I frowned. She was right. No matter how psycho she was, I'd never risk my child's life simply because I loathed the woman who'd given birth to him.

"I want to see him."

She shook her head. "I can't let you do that."

"Excuse me?" I placed my hands flat on the table, then fell silent as the waiter put down our food. After he walked away, I continued, "You come to me, tell me I have a six-year-old son who I never knew anything about, talk about how you weren't being fair to him by keeping him a secret, and then ask me for money, but I can't see him?"

"I can't let you into his life if you're going to just abandon him again."

"There's no again here, Sasha. I didn't abandon him in the first place. I didn't know he existed." I fought to keep my voice calm. Yelling wasn't going to solve anything.

"Come on, DeVon. We both know you're not the kind of guy who sticks around. How can I know you won't hurt him? Spend a couple weeks with him and then decide you're bored. I can't let you discard him like you did me. I need to know you are going to be a part of our lives before I let you in."

Our lives. Shit. That didn't sound good.

"We were good together, DeVon," Sasha said as she leaned across the table towards me. "Don't you remember? That last night...how amazing it was? All the things I did for you. The things you did to me. We can have that again. All of that, and more, because this time, we have Emmett to keep us together."

Against my better judgment, the memories of that night flooded forward and I couldn't help but remember it all, including the person I'd been back then, the one before I'd met Krissy.

# TEN
## DEVON

I'd stopped using my hand to spank her when my palm started hurting, but her skin still wasn't that pretty shade of deep red that meant it was going to bruise and that's what I wanted.

And Sasha was all about giving me what I wanted.

When I'd met her a week before, I'd taken one look at those curves and had known that I'd be fucking her by the end of the night. We hadn't even made it that long. Less than twenty minutes after she'd told me her name, she'd proven what I'd suspected from moment one. That mouth had been made for sucking cock.

The seven days that followed had been filled with one depravity after another. All I had to do was mention it and she'd do it. She never wanted it gentle, which was good because I didn't do that. I made her come, of course. I always made my girls come. But she kept asking me for more, as if wanting to prove that she was my perfect Sub.

She'd gone down on me under a table at one of LA's finest restaurants. Let me tie her up in all sorts of positions. I'd used dozens of different toys on her. Spent three hours making her come until she was so sensitive that even a breath of air was too much. Spent two hours edging her and then sent her home with instructions to masturbate every hour but not to come until I saw her again that evening. She'd come the moment I entered her and had almost squeezed my dick right off. I'd fucked her mouth, her cunt, her ass, used toys in her ass while I fucked her pussy and vice versa. I'd spanked her, used nipple clamps, a flogger.

Then there was today. I'd mentioned at some point during all of the fucking that I'd yet to fuck a woman with a clit piercing. A half hour ago, she'd showed up at my apartment wearing only a trench coat. She'd opened it in the hallway, parted her legs and then spread her lips with her fingers, showing me the swollen bundle of nerves that now had a shiny silver hoop through it.

That should've been my first clue that her eagerness to please was bordering on dangerous.

Instead of getting a clue, however, my blood had rushed straight to my cock and I'd told her that she'd gotten pierced without my permission and she'd need to be punished. That's when I'd started spanking her with my hand. Then I'd switched to a crop. Now, I was going to push her further than before.

"Turn over," I said.

She immediately did as I said, wincing as she laid on her back.

"Spread your legs."

She obeyed.

I slapped the crop against my hand, the sound echoing in the spare room. My apartment wasn't quite as big as the penthouse I wanted eventually, but I at least had one room to sleep in and another to play in. I waited until her eyes were following the crop before flicking out my wrist.

She screamed as the tip of the crop hit directly at the place where her clit had been pierced. She writhed on the bed, unable to put her hands between her legs to protect her sensitive flesh. Her wrists were bound together by silk. If she pulled too hard, the cloth would start to cut into her flesh. Her ankles weren't bound, however, and her legs kicked.

I waited for her to quit moving, enjoying the way her breasts jiggled with the movement. Her nipples were already swollen, the tips jutting up, having been bitten and pulled until they were impossibly hard. My mouth had left other marks across the tanned flesh.

This time, I made sure the flat of the crop was what came in contact with her clit. Her back arched and her mouth opened, but no sound came out. I put the crop down and watched. There was only so much abuse certain body parts could suffer without permanent damage and I never did anything like that. She'd be feeling all of this for a while, but I didn't want to truly harm her.

When she finally fell back on the bed, legs splayed open side, I climbed onto the bed. I stretched out and, without any preamble, began to run my tongue over the piercing, the metallic taste mingling with Sasha's own musky flavor. Whimpers fell from her lips as I focused all of my attention on her sore clit. I licked and sucked until she finally came, the stimulation too much for her to handle. Her entire body went limp as she passed out. I used the time to roll a condom over my stiff cock.

A shudder passed over her as I started to slide into her. I'd purposefully avoided paying any attention to her pussy, leaving her dripping, but tight. I went as fast as I could without hurting myself, watching the strain of initial penetration play across her face. When I came to rest inside her, I leaned forward until the base of my cock pressed against her clit.

She cried out, her hands tugging at her restraints. I maintained my position as I started to move. Every thrust rubbed against that spot inside her, but also pressed against her clit with what had to be painful pressure. When I sped up, she began to beg me to finish.

"I'm not even close," I said. I could've gone if I'd just given up control, but that wasn't about to happen any time soon.

"My ass," she gasped as I pushed against her clit. "Fuck my ass, please. Anything that leaves my clit alone."

I pulled out and she gave a half-sob of relief. I reached up and tugged on her restraints. The knots holding her gave and she dropped her arms. She rubbed at her wrists and I saw that they were red, almost raw. She'd wear the marks for a few days before they finally disappeared. But that wasn't my concern.

"Bend your legs up to your chest," I instructed.

She gave me a puzzled look but did as I said.

"Grab your thighs."

She did.

"As long as you hold your legs up, I'm going to fuck your ass, but as soon as you drop them, I'm going back to your pussy and I'm going to rub your clit with my thumb until I come." I gave her a moment to absorb it. "Did you prep yourself before you came?"

She nodded.

I always made sure the women I fucked knew to be prepared at all times. If they forgot, it was their fault if it hurt. They could always safe word and walk away. I made sure they all knew that. Nothing happened to any of them that they didn't agree to take. If they didn't like it but said nothing, that wasn't my fault.

I teased the tip of my cock against her entrance before sliding down lower and positioning it at her asshole. I'd taken her ass a couple of times so I knew how much she could take at once. Tonight, however, I tested those limits and shoved myself inside with one thrust. Before she'd even stopping wailing, I was pounding into her. Her body was nearly bent in two and she begged for me to fuck her harder.

When I was close, I pulled out and earned a pained yelp. I pulled off the condom and tossed it towards the trashcan specifically positioned for moments such as this. I began to fist my cock rapidly, pushing myself towards orgasm. It didn't take long. With a grunt, I came, spurting my semen across her belly and tits. I closed my eyes as the last of my cum dripped onto her body.

I sat back on my heels and let my breathing slow before I opened my eyes. She was watching me, licking her fingers.

"That was hot," she said. She pushed herself up into a half-seated position, resting more on her hip than her ass.

I made a non-committal noise and climbed off of the bed. I went into the guest bathroom and wiped myself off before going back into the bedroom.

Sasha had crawled under the covers and left them pulled back on one side of the bed. She patted the mattress. "Come on, babe. I'm exhausted."

I gave her a scornful look. "You know I don't do the whole afterglow thing."

Her expression tightened. She ran her fingers over her breasts. "You marked me," she said. "Claimed me. I'm yours."

Oh, shit. I hadn't realized she'd gone that far. Usually, there were more warning signs and I was able to recognize them before real feelings grew.

"I marked you," I agreed. "But I'm not claiming anything. Or anyone."

Her eyes narrowed and she sat up straight.

"I made it perfectly clear when this began that I didn't do relationships. We fuck for a couple weeks and that's it. Maybe the occasional hook-up if I have an itch to scratch, but that's it. No one is claiming anyone here."

"Fuck you," she snapped.

She climbed out of bed and stormed around the side to stand directly in front of me, so close that her nipples were almost touching me. If I'd been erect, my cock would've been pushing against her.

"I did everything for you." She practically spat the words into my face. "I was your little fuck-toy and never said no. You need me."

I laughed and turned away from her. "You think I don't have a dozen women who'd take your place in a second?"

"You bastard!" she yelled.

Something hit me in the back of the head and I turned. Her eyes were blazing and there was a pillow at my feet, one of the decorative ones my interior designer had purchased for whatever reason.

"Okay, this has gone far enough," I said, all humor gone. "Get out."

"You can't throw me out!" She stomped her foot like a child. "When a couple fights, they work it out and make up. One of them doesn't throw the other one out."

"We're not a couple, Sasha," I said. "What's it going to take for you to get that? I'll call security if I have to and I tip well enough that they won't think twice about dragging you out of here completely naked." I wasn't so sure that was true, but it was a threat I doubted I'd need to follow through with.

"Fine," she snapped.

She marched out into the living room and I followed to make sure she was actually going to go. I was starting to think if I didn't see her walk out the door and then lock it behind her, she'd pop up in the shower later on. I was really going to have to pay better attention to other women in the future. The second they started getting too into things, I was going to have to begin looking for a time to opt out.

"This isn't over," Sasha said as she pulled her coat back on and pulled on her shoes. "We're meant to be together, DeVon. You'll see."

"No." I shook my head. "We're not. You walk out that door and that's the last time I want to see you."

She gave me an enigmatic smile. "You don't mean that. Not really. And when you come to your senses, I'll be there, waiting. I won't let you go, sweetheart."

As I shut and locked the door behind her, I had a bad feeling that I was going to have to get a restraining order against her. At least if it came to that, it would be the end. If she violated it, she'd be arrested. A couple nights in jail and she'd forget all about me. I gave it a couple weeks, tops, and then I'd never hear from Sasha Richmond again. I was sure of it.

## ELEVEN

## KRISSY

After having such a great time in New York, I'd expected the first full week back home, getting back in the real world routine, would be rough. I just hadn't realized how rough. Aside from feeling like crap almost the entire time and whatever it was going on with DeVon, I also had this whole Landon thing hanging over my head. I spent the last two days of the week attempting to catch up on what I'd missed while I'd been out, but it had been difficult focusing, especially since I couldn't seem to get DeVon alone long enough to ask him if everything was okay and where he'd been on Wednesday.

Of course, his silence worried me, which didn't do anything to help the anxiety eating at me. I had to admit that there was a part of me that was starting to fear that he was getting bored with our relationship. I knew that this relationship was the longest one either of us had ever had. Usually, we were the fuck 'em and leave 'em type. He'd told me that, with the exception of Haley, he'd rarely been with a woman for more than a few weeks. For me, it was a couple months per guy. Neither one of us had lasted almost a year before now.

The longevity of our relationship scared the shit out of me, but in that good kind of way. The kind that said maybe I finally had found what everyone was always talking about, that one true love. He was the only person I'd ever been able to see a future with. When I thought about planning another trip to New York next year, it didn't freak me out that I assumed I'd be going with him. I thought about holidays with him. The two of us growing old together. And it didn't make me want to run for the hills. That was new.

In the past, whenever I'd looked into the future and had seen myself doing something with someone, it had always been a faceless stranger, no matter who I was with at the time. I'd always assumed I'd be with a new person by the time whatever plans I was thinking about making came to pass. And, until DeVon, it had been true.

I'd never really thought anything of it. Some of my friends, like Carrie, had always seen themselves as eventually ending up in a long-term relationship, but I never had. Honestly, I'd been blind-sided when I'd realized that's what I wanted with DeVon. I hadn't started shopping for wedding dresses or baby clothes or anything, but he was the first man I'd ever thought of as being in it for the long haul.

And I'd thought he felt the same way. Now, I wasn't so sure. He wasn't being cruel or dropping hints that he wanted to end things, but neither of those things were really his style. Since our little misunderstanding with Carter Bilson, DeVon and I had made it a point to always be honest with each other. Did it lead to some heated arguments? Yes. But it had also led to the hottest make-up sex I'd ever had. I'd always assumed that if things were going to end with us, he would just come out and say it. I didn't think that was the case, and I didn't even want to consider it, but I didn't have any evidence that it could be anything else. More than that, I couldn't think of another reason he'd be behaving this way.

I tried telling myself it was work distracting him, but I knew that wasn't a real possibility. DeVon worked hard, but he also played hard. For all the time he spent at the office, I'd never seen him choose work over us. It was one of the things we had in common. Sure, we put in overtime when we needed to. It was a business and sometimes stuff like that was needed, but we never let it get in the way of personal time, even if it was just an hour or two a day, and we ended up falling asleep mid-sentence.

This week, however, he'd barely spoken to me what little time we'd seen each other and he hadn't once tried to initiate sex. At first, I'd thought it was because I hadn't been feeling well, but even after I'd told him I was feeling better, he hadn't tried anything. I supposed, for some people, that a week without sex wasn't strange, but for DeVon and I, we at least spent some time in some sort of physical contact several times a week. With the exception of Monday night, he'd barely touched me.

I figured that once the weekend rolled around, I'd finally get the chance to spend some time with him and we could talk about what was going on. Except, I woke up Saturday morning and he was gone. The note said he was at the gym, and that wasn't very unusual. What was strange, however, was that he didn't come home around noon, smelling like a fresh shower and take me into the bedroom for other calorie-burning activities. That had been his routine on the other days when he'd gone into the gym.

Instead, I spent the day lazing about the house, trying to find something to do while I waited for him to come home. I was strangely restless, as if my body knew something was up even if my head didn't want to admit it. I wandered from room to room, finding little things to straighten or clean even though house-keeping came through twice a week. I thought about different things I'd like to change and tried making a mental list of them, only to forget my ideas a room or two later.

When he finally came home, he looked exhausted and the smile he gave me was weak. I asked him if everything was okay and he just nodded and headed off to the bathroom. A few minutes later, I heard the shower turn on.

I sighed. I was at a loss. I wanted to talk to him about what was going on with him. I wanted to talk to him about the whole Landon situation and the proposal Mayflower had made. Every time I opened my mouth, however, he basically shut me down. I considered being blunt, but I knew DeVon. If he didn't want to talk about it, he wouldn't. It wouldn't matter how things were approached. He'd just find a way to change the subject or ignore it altogether. I was willing to bet that if I asked him outright what I should do about Landon or even told him Mayflower's proposal, he'd give me a "whatever you feel is best" kind of answer. When he was wrapped up in his head, nothing could break through.

He didn't go anywhere Sunday, but every attempt at conversation was rebuffed. First, it was because he wanted to relax and read the paper. Next, he reminded me that I'd said I'd handle the whole Landon situation and he wanted me to do just that. As I'd assumed the night before, he assured me that he trusted my judgment in the matter. He said he had too much going on in his head to worry about Landon, too. I asked what else was happening and he didn't answer. As far as we were concerned, the conversation was over.

By Monday morning, I was two days away from needing to give Mayflower an answer or the shit was going to hit the fan. There were only two people in the entire agency that I could trust to handle things with discretion if I presented them with my conundrum, even in hypotheticals. One was DeVon's assistant Melissa, and I knew that involving her would put her in an awkward position because there was no way she wouldn't figure out what was really going on, especially since she knew something was up with Landon. The other person I could trust was Tracy, my personal assistant. I knew she was loyal to the agency and to DeVon, but she was more loyal to me. If I asked her something hypothetically and told her not to talk to anyone about it, she wouldn't feel guilty if she kept it from DeVon.

After lunch, I stopped next to Tracy's desk instead of continuing on into my office.

"What's up?" she asked as she looked up from her computer screen.

"That obvious?" I asked grimly. While I considered Melissa a friend, Tracy was the only woman on the West Coast I really felt comfortable confiding in. She wasn't quite as good as having Carrie here, but I was willing to bet that once she and I knew each other for a few more years, we'd be just as close.

She nodded. "Something was up with you all last week. You and DeVon both."

"Did you hear something about DeVon?" I asked.

She shook her head this time. "I just know that the two of you used to always be flirting with each other and finding all sorts of little excuses to see each other. Last week, I don't think I saw the two of you together at all." She frowned, thinking. "In fact, I'm not sure I saw DeVon at all." She gave me a concerned look. "Are you guys fighting?"

"No," I said. Then I sighed. "Or if we are, I don't know about it. He's been just as weird at home."

"But you're not stopping by to chat about DeVon acting strange, are you?"

"No, I have another problem I need some help thinking through solutions for." I leaned against the edge of her desk. "I can't give you specifics, but I have a hypothetical situation that's similar in the aspects that matter."

"All right." She leaned back in her chair. "Shoot."

"A photographer is trying to blackmail a Mirage client with

pictures of said client engaged in activity that would tarnish his or her career," I began. "The photographer wants an obscene amount of money that Mirage isn't willing to pay. When threatened with legal action should the aforementioned photographs be released, the photographer offers to cut the amount in half – which is a much more reasonable sum – if one of Mirage's employees performs a sexual act."

"Well," Tracy said, leaning forward now and placing her elbows on the desk. "If I was that employee, I'd probably punch the photographer in the nose and damn the consequences, but I'm pretty sure that's not a legitimate option."

"Unfortunately, it's not," I said with a half-smile.

"I can't really say what the employee should do since I'm not the one being asked, and we all know how often tits and ass are used to get things done in this town," she continued. "But, I can say that I've heard rumors that this wouldn't be the first time that someone from Mirage would've done something like that."

"Really?" I was surprised I hadn't heard those rumors before. I knew Mirage's employees were discreet, but something like that seemed like it'd be difficult to keep under wraps.

Tracy nodded. "A couple years back, there was this studio exec, some shrew of a woman, who was threatening to fire one of Mirage's clients for some political stance the actor had taken. DeVon went in and, four hours later, the actor wasn't fired and the executive never threatened Mirage again. The rumor is that the woman told DeVon if he had sex with her, it'd all go away."

If this had been a recent rumor, I would've disregarded it because I knew DeVon would never cheat on me, but a couple years ago, he probably wouldn't have even thought twice. If that had indeed been the offer, I had no doubt that he'd done it, and had probably had her begging for more.

"Thanks, Tracy." I managed a tired smile. "Anything new come in while I was at lunch?"

"Nope." She turned back to her computer. "And your three o'clock appointment had to reschedule for next week. Something about a Botox injection gone wrong so she had to go to the ER."

I rolled my eyes. That didn't surprise me. Mirage encouraged their clients to stay away from 'treatments' not being given out by a respected practitioner, but some people didn't listen. "Thanks."

My rescheduled appointment faded from my mind as I refocused on the problem at hand. What DeVon had done had been before we'd gotten together, but he'd also been the one who'd told me that Hollywood ran on tits and ass. He'd hated thinking that Carter Bilson and I had slept together so much so that he'd nearly ruined everything between us – and we hadn't officially been a couple at that point. I doubted he'd ever tell me to 'take one for the team' again.

I sat down in my chair and pulled up my email even though I wasn't really looking at it. The problem was, this wasn't just about Mirage or a single client. Landon was a friend and this could ruin him, not only professionally, but personally as well. Could I really let my friend lose everything he'd ever worked for simply because I didn't want to perform an act I'd done hundreds of times in the past? I'd never gotten paid for sex, but I had received some nice gifts from men I'd fucked, and I'd sometimes 'repaid a favor' with a blow-job or hand-job. Was this really any different?

It was hard to compare the two, I knew, but it wasn't thinking about having sex with Mayflower to protect Landon that was the problem. Sure, I found the man disgusting and the thought of him touching me made me want to vomit, but those were physical reactions.

No, what I was worried about was what this would do to DeVon and my relationship. I could try to keep it a secret, but it'd come to light eventually and having lied about it would just make things worse. But the idea of telling him terrified me. I knew how vulnerable he was when it came to things like this. Catching his fiancée in bed with his best friend two days after he proposed had really fucked him up when it came to trusting women. If I did this, there was a very good chance I'd lose him.

I just didn't see any other way out. Landon wasn't only my friend, he was DeVon's friend, and I couldn't let this happen to him when I had the power to stop it. I had one last ditch hope before I agreed, however. I'd call Mayflower, I decided, and tell him that I would be convincing DeVon to pay the full million. Once I told DeVon what the options were, I was sure he'd agree to the money rather than me. I didn't know if Mayflower would go back to the original terms.

First, I called Landon. No matter what offer was accepted, Mayflower would be bought off and my friend would be safe. I didn't want Landon spending any more time worrying. He didn't answer, so I left a vague message telling him it'd be handled and breathed a sigh of relief that I didn't have to try to dance my way around any questions he threw my way.

My next call was to Mayflower to give him my counter offer.

"I see how it is," he said when I'd finished. "You think you're too good for me. You'll parade around at your fancy parties, flirting and showing off. Probably fucking anyone up there who wants you, just to get your company flying high. But me, no, I don't get that same treatment."

I wanted to ask him if he'd always been a moron or if someone had dropped him on his head as a child, but I refrained and let him keep talking even though it didn't sound like he was liking what I'd said.

"A million's not on the table anymore," he said. "Three million cash, or half a million and I get to fuck you. Quarter of a million if you bring along a couple of your prettiest clients to join us."

It was on the tip of my tongue to tell him to go fuck himself and it took all of my self-control not to do it. We couldn't give him three million in cash. It wasn't that we couldn't get it together in time. If we gave him that much money, it'd be open season on our clients. Every paparazzi in Hollywood would be trying to find compromising pictures they could use to blackmail us and our people.

"You sign an NDA that states you never speak about what you saw, the pictures you took or the arrangement we come to," I said. "There will also be a legally binding addendum that prohibits you from photographing, recording or otherwise bene-fiting from any images of any Mirage clients ever again."

"You can't do that," he sputtered. "I got a right to take pictures of who I want."

"You do and I'll go public with the fact that you not only blackmailed Mirage for money, but for sex as well."

"No one'll care," he retorted.

"They will if I mention that you wanted me to bring Mirage's youngest female clients along to join in the fun."

"I never said that! I ain't no pervert."

That was debatable, I supposed, but I kept my observation to myself. "Once you sign the agreement that I'll draw up, you get half a million dollars." The words were rancid in my mouth. "And you get me."

By the time Wednesday arrived, I was a wreck. Pale, dark circles under my eyes. I hadn't eaten because the nausea had returned full force. Tracy kept asking if I was coming down with something, but DeVon didn't notice, or at least didn't mention anything if he had. I was more convinced than ever that he was trying to figure out how to break off our personal relationship without affecting our professional one. He wouldn't want me to leave Mirage. I was too much a part of who the agency was now. I'd brought in clients of my own who would go with me if I left. Not to mention people like Lena Dunn and Cami Matthews, my first clients who were now regular guest stars on two established TV shows.

All of that on top of what I'd agreed to do with Mayflower was killing me. It didn't help matters that I knew as soon as DeVon found out what I'd done, it would most likely solidify his decision about our relationship. If I hadn't been so unsure about where we were, I might've been a bit more confident that he'd see the necessity behind what I was going to do, but now, I wasn't so sure.

I'd spent all day yesterday perfecting the contract I was

going to make Mayflower sign. It was ironclad and made it so that if he so much as breathed in the direction of one of our clients or hinted at anything that had transpired over the past week, he'd be libel not only for monetary compensation to the wronged party, but also criminal charges as the details of the arrangement would become public knowledge. I also buried a couple things in there regarding threats to out any celebrity, even those not represented by Mirage. After today, I'd be watching him like a hawk and the second he violated a single word of this contract, I was going to nail his ass to the wall. He could yell and scream First Amendment all he wanted, but a judge would have to uphold the contract. It'd be on Mayflower's head if he didn't read it, and considering he'd be signing it before he got to fuck me, I had a feeling he wasn't going to bother reading it since I'd told him that I was going to make him sign an NDA that I wrote. It wasn't my responsibility to disclose every detail of the document to him.

The thought of being able to outsmart this asshole was all that kept me going as I headed towards the part of LA where there were 'massage' parlors and hotels that rented rooms by the hour. Mayflower had set up the place and I had a feeling I wasn't the first woman who'd been coerced into fucking him in one of these rooms.

As I approached, he turned towards me and I wanted so badly to wipe that shit-eating grin off of his face. Instead, I held out the envelope with the contract in it.

"What's this?" he asked.

"The NDA you're going to sign before you get what's in this bag." I patted the bag I was carrying. "And before you get any closer to me than where you are now."

He scowled at me as he pulled out the papers. "Got a pen?"

I handed him a pen and waited to see if he'd hurry through

or actually read the pages he was signing. Before he could do either one, however, I heard my name being called.

"Krissy! Don't you dare!"

I turned to see Landon walking quickly across the parking lot, his expression angrier than I'd ever seen it before.

"Landon, you shouldn't be here." My hands tightened on the strap of the bag.

"No fuck." He grabbed the papers out of Mayflower's hand and shoved them back at me. "Whatever deal you've made, it's off."

"Mind your own business, you fucking fa—"

Landon grabbed the front of Mayflower's shirt and lifted the short man up onto his toes. My jaw dropped as Landon slammed the reporter against the side of the hotel.

"Listen to me, you piss-poor excuse for a human being." His blue eyes flashed. "I've had it with you and your kind thinking the First Amendment was written so you could make money off of prying into people's personal lives and acting like it's news. You're going to stay the hell away from me and if I see so much as a hint of those pictures, I'll see to it that the only job you can get is sucking dick for gay porn." He shoved Mayflower away. "Now get out of here."

For a moment, I thought Mayflower was going to try to retaliate and that I'd have to call the cops on a fight I really didn't want to see in the papers, but something about the way Landon was holding himself said that he wasn't joking about any of it.

After Mayflower took off, Landon turned to me. "What the hell are you thinking, Krissy?!"

I stared at him, unable to believe what had just happened.

"When I got your message, I started doing some research and I heard from a couple different people the kinds of 'deals' Mayflower made. It didn't take much to figure out where he would've taken you. I'm just glad I got here in time."

"You and me both," I said. I wrapped my arms around myself, suddenly cold despite the stifling heat. "Do you really think he's going to sit on those pictures?"

Landon shrugged. "Probably not for long, but I'm going to beat him to the punch."

My eyebrows went up and I wondered if I was misunderstanding what he was saying.

"When I wasn't tracking down information on Mayflower, I was coming to grips with this decision." Landon squared his shoulders and took a deep breath. "I made some calls and I have an exclusive interview with Proud and Out magazine on Friday. I'm through hiding."

"That's great!" I threw my arms around him, feeling tears pricking at my eyelids. As relief rushed through me, the tears escaped and I began to sob, everything that had happened in the last week and a half pouring out in one gigantic flood of emotion.

"Hey, hey, it's okay." Landon hugged me close. "Shh, sweetie. It's all right."

"No." I shook my head. "It's not." I tried to stem the flow of tears, but they just kept coming. What the hell was wrong with me? Sure, this was a lot of shit going on, but I'd dealt with worse.

"Come here." He took my arm and led me back to his car. It was nice, but not overtly flashy. He waited until the air cooled us both down a bit before turning to me. "Now, what's wrong, hon?"

I hesitated for a moment, but when Landon reached over and took my hand, the kind gesture completely undid me and everything came pouring out. Mayflower's proposal. DeVon's strange behavior. How he hadn't even noticed that I hadn't been sleeping or eating.

"You know him," I said. I took a shuddering breath. "He's

never done a long-term relationship, not since Haley. What if he's getting bored with me?"

"Krissy, don't be silly." Landon plucked a tissue from a box and wiped my eyes. "DeVon is madly in love with you. He has been since before he'd admit it to anyone, including himself."

"But what if he's falling out of love with me?" I pressed the issue. "What if the reason he's been so distant is that he doesn't know how to tell me it's over?" I let all of my fears spill out.

Landon grasped both of my hands between his. "Look at me."

I did, my eyes meeting his.

"I have known DeVon for years and I've seen him with dozens of different women, but from the moment he met you, he's been a different person. A better person. He's not going to give you up."

"But he's being so distant." My insides twisted as I thought of all the times over the past week-and-a-half where I'd tried to be close to him and he'd pulled away or ignored me. The times when I'd thought he'd be concerned about me, but he'd barely acknowledged my existence.

"Krissy Jensen." Landon's voice was firm. "You are one of the strongest women I know, so get off your ass and do something about it."

I blinked. I hadn't been expecting that.

"Do you love him?"

"More than anything." The answer was automatic. I didn't even have to think about it.

"Then fight for him. Go after him. Make him tell you what's wrong. Do not give in without a fight. That's one of the things he loves the most about you," Landon said. "Did you know that? We've talked sex and love over the years, so I know a bit about his fetishes and preferences. He likes to be the dominant person in a relationship, but I also know that he loves it when you push back, when you challenge him. Your strength is what drew him to you in the first place."

I sniffled and reached for another tissue. I didn't feel particularly strong at the moment.

"If you love him, fight." Landon kissed my forehead. "Now, let's get a manicure and go shopping. I have to look perfect for my interview on Friday and you should get some sexy new lingerie that DeVon can tear off with his teeth."

# THIRTEEN
## KRISSY

After spending the day with Landon, I was feeling much better when I got home. I considered putting on the barely-there lingerie I'd gotten and greeting DeVon at the door, but eventually decided against it. I wasn't entirely sure when he'd been getting home and I wanted to talk to him about what was going on before working on any seduction. In the end, it turned out to be the right choice because I ended up falling asleep on the couch before he got home.

I woke up in the middle of the night to find the house dark. I was covered with a blanket, which was a nice gesture on DeVon's part, but it didn't sit quite right with me. On the rare occasion in the past when I'd fallen asleep, DeVon had carried me to our bed. I supposed he could've been too tired, but I suspected it was more that he hadn't wanted to risk waking me and having me ask him what was going on.

I went into the bathroom on the main level and turned on the shower. I needed time to think and the hot water would ease the kinks out of my back. I knew he wouldn't hear me down here. It was obvious that DeVon wasn't going to talk to me. I'd tried and he'd had plenty of opportunities. I hated the idea of sneaking around behind his back, but it looked like he wasn't giving me much of a choice.

By the time I finished my shower, I'd made my decision. I quietly crept into the bedroom and got some clothes, then went back to the living room. I dressed in the jeans and t-shirt and crawled back under the blanket to attempt to get a couple more hours sleep before DeVon left.

I heard him a few hours later, moving about in the kitchen and trying not to make any noise. I feigned sleep, wondering if he'd come in and kiss me good-bye like he usually did when he left before me. Instead, I heard the front door close.

I got up quickly and slipped on the shoes I'd placed by the couch. I wondered if he would've even noticed that I'd changed or that I had shoes ready even if he had come in. As distracted as I'd been, I doubted it.

I opened the front door carefully and saw DeVon pulling out of the driveway. As soon as he was out of sight, I hurried to my car, pulling up my GPS app as I went. DeVon and I both had 'find me' apps on our phones since so much of our business information was on them. I'd never dreamed I'd be using it to track him.

I followed the blinking dot, keeping myself close enough that I could still catch glimpses of his car but far enough that he wouldn't be able to see me. I'd admit to following him when I finally confronted him, but I wanted to be sure I knew what was going on before I did anything.

Eventually, we ended up at the Pan Pacific Park. Now I was really confused. I'd been prepared to follow him into a lawyer's office, to a hotel for some liaison, even to a restaurant to meet with a lawyer or a woman. Hell, I wouldn't have been surprised if we'd gone to some sort of sex club. A park hadn't even been anywhere near the list I'd been making in my head.

I parked several spaces away and waited until I saw him get

out before I did the same. I'd purposefully picked plain clothes and had my hair pulled back in a ponytail so I wouldn't draw any attention to myself. Now I saw that he had done the same thing. There wasn't really much of a way for him to disguise those powerful shoulders or his height, but he'd worn a pair of plain jeans and a t-shirt that wasn't fitted to show off his physique. Basically, he'd worn what he usually wore to do work around the house. While he usually hired people to do things like that, every once in a while, he'd get in the mood to fix or do something himself. That was one of the outfits he wore.

He couldn't be meeting someone here for an affair, not dressed like that. And I doubted he'd be talking to the press for any reason, especially not a clandestine meet like this. I frowned as I followed him, always keeping a few feet back as he headed deeper into the park.

When he finally stopped, he stuck his hands in his pockets and looked around as if he was waiting for someone. I ducked behind a tree, aware that anyone who saw me would know that I was spying on someone. I didn't care, though. Whoever he was meeting here had to be the reason he'd been acting so strangely and missing so much work lately. I'd called Tracy to tell her I'd be working in the field today and I had no doubt that DeVon had made a similar call to Melissa. I wondered if he'd told her he was working or just that he wouldn't be coming in. All I knew was that I wasn't the only one he'd been lying to.

After a few minutes, a woman came towards him. She had dark hair and tanned skin, a build similar to mine. We didn't look enough alike that people would think we were related, but I didn't doubt he'd dated her. Or what had passed for dating DeVon at one point. Unless – my stomach did a flip – he was fucking her now, and the fact that she and I had some of the same physical characteristics was part of his attraction.

I shook away the thought. I'd seen DeVon with plenty of

women before we'd gotten together as well as after. His body language had changed once we'd become official. Before, he hadn't just oozed charm and sex appeal, he'd used both like a weapon. Women had been conquests, whether they'd realized it or not. Now, even when he was using those same qualities, it was different. There was an acknowledgement that it was business only, that there wouldn't be any follow-through because he was taken. I knew that's how it came across, because I did the same thing. We'd flirt, but we always went home together.

I watched him with the woman and read his body language since I wasn't close enough to hear what they were saying. DeVon wasn't angling himself towards her or trying to get closer. If anything, he was presenting himself in a very stand-offish kind of way. I felt better...until she stepped into his personal space and put her hand on his arm. When he didn't shrug her off or move back, all of the previously dispelled tension returned.

Then I saw her motion for someone to come over and I followed the line of sight. A dark-haired boy, maybe six or seven years old, walked over from where he'd been playing. He walked over to DeVon, a serious expression on his young face. He didn't look like DeVon or the woman, not really, but I still had a bad feeling I knew what was going on.

My stomach lurched and I fought back the urge to vomit. I hadn't eaten anything yet this morning and I was glad that I hadn't. I was pretty sure it would've made a re-appearance.

I closed my eyes for a moment and focused on breathing. I was a lawyer, I reminded myself. I might not have really practiced law in the past year and I might've specialized in divorces, but I still had that lawyer mind-set. Evidence. Proof. I couldn't jump to conclusions just because of how things looked.

I thought back to what had happened when DeVon had made an assumption based on how things had looked. Based on innuendos over a meal, he'd thought I was going to Carter Bilson's house to sleep with him in order to get a couple clients to read for a movie. When he'd arrived at the director's house, I'd answered the door in a robe, hair wet from a shower. All of the evidence had pointed towards the logical conclusion that I'd fucked Bilson, when in reality, I'd gotten into a car accident, called Bilson to pick me up because I'd been pissed at DeVon, and had taken a shower at the director's house to clean up. Bilson had propositioned me, but I'd turned him down. Of course, on the surface, it hadn't looked that way.

For all I knew, the boy was DeVon's nephew and the woman was his brother Franco's ex. After all, I'd slept with Franco back in New York, so he obviously liked curvier brunettes, too. Or she could be some random woman accusing one of our clients of something. There were a plethora of possibilities and I didn't have proof to support or disprove any of them.

I opened my eyes and pulled out my phone. I peeked around the tree and saw that the woman was laughing, her hand on DeVon's chest. I couldn't see his face, but his body looked stiff, which I took to mean he wasn't appreciating the affection. That was good. I still didn't like the woman, whoever she was, but I was less suspicious that DeVon was sleeping with her. If anything, he appeared to be more interested in the boy than the woman.

I snapped a couple pictures of the woman and put my phone back in my pocket. I'd teased Carrie about how she'd gone from a lawyer to a private investigator over the last year-and-a-half as she'd started looking into the whole sex trafficking industry, but I was going to do the same. Well, not for something as noble as my friend. No, I was going to find out who this woman was and how she was connected to DeVon. And I knew just the place to start.

I headed over to the precinct a few blocks over. About six

months ago, one of Mirage's clients had gotten arrested for public intoxication and resisting arrest. I'd gone to the station and spoken with the arresting officer. I'd been honest and explained how Taylor, a young man I knew well, had just found out that his nineteen-year-old brother had been killed in action overseas earlier that day. I hadn't asked for the charges to be dropped, just that the officer take the circumstances into consideration when determining the next step. Officer Purdue had voided the arrest and let Taylor go. Since then, Officer Purdue and I had become, while not exactly friends, buddies. He kept me informed of any problems with Mirage clients as they happened and I never asked for special treatment. I also helped talk his daughter into staying in law school instead of dropping out to pursue a career in acting by promising her that if she passed the bar, Mirage would represent her should she still want to be an actress.

Today, I was going to ask for a real favor.

Officer Purdue was a tough-looking, heavy-set man with the kind of face that most people wouldn't remember. He was also much smarter than people gave him credit for, which was probably why he was so good at his job. He took advantage of the fact that most people thought he was of average intelligence and usually ended up showing them up.

It took me a couple minutes to track him down, but when I did, he gave me a warm smile and invited me to have a seat while he did some paperwork.

"How's Raina doing?" I asked. I was itching to get to the real reason why I was here, but I wasn't going to be rude. Besides, if it hadn't been for the current situation, I would've been genuinely interested in his daughter's progress at Columbia.

"Made the Dean's List last semester," he said. "And she took your advice and went down to see your friend about putting in some volunteer hours."

I'd actually known that. Carrie had told me she'd hired Raina and that things were going well. I was glad. Raina had the talent to be an actress but I wasn't sure she had the right temperament.

"What about you?" he asked as he moved on to a new stack of forms. "I've been hearing rumors that something's been going on at Mirage."

"Really?" I sat forward, momentarily distracted from my own problem.

"A couple hookers we brought in last night said they saw someone who looked a lot like Landon Sully threatening Garrison Mayflower. Maybe even assaulting him."

Shit. I hadn't realized anyone had seen what had happened at the motel.

"Not that I could blame Sully if that were true," Officer Purdue continued. "Mayflower's a cockroach. Puts shit out there and then hides behind the Constitution like calling himself a reporter gives him the excuse to ruin people's lives or put someone in danger."

There was no love lost between Mayflower and the LAPD. Last year, he'd published a piece about police brutality that had been based on an unfounded rumor, had refused to disclose his source and kept writing about how he was being harassed for writing the truth. Two cops were killed because of the article and, when an investigation revealed that Mayflower's source had been lying through her teeth, there had been no retraction or apology.

"Are you going to be investigating the accusations?" I asked. I knew what the most likely answer was, but I wouldn't relax until I heard it from Purdue himself.

"Mayflower hasn't come in to file charges," Officer Purdue said. "Probably knows we wouldn't take him very seriously if he did." He glanced at me. "Still, you might want to let Sully know that it's possible the hookers will say something to someone about what they saw."

"Thanks for the head's up," I said. With Landon coming out soon, we'd probably have to look out for people trying to cash in and a pair of hookers were a likely bet to try to do just that.

"I'm guessing you didn't come here just to shoot the breeze with me," Purdue said.

"No, I didn't." I took my phone out of my pocket and pulled up the pictures I'd taken. "I need to talk with our legal department if she's accusing the company of something." I paused, and then added, "And if it's personal, I need to know that, too."

Officer Purdue didn't ask me why I wasn't asking DeVon about the woman, and I was grateful. His discretion was another reason why I liked him.

"Send me the pictures," he said. "I'll run her, but I can't make any promises."

"I know," I said. "But I'd rather have you doing this instead of bringing someone in to investigate and not knowing if I can trust them."

"I'm assuming you want me to call you directly with the results," he said.

I nodded. "That would be great. Anything you can find. Name. Where she's from. If she has any prior connection to Mirage. Any legal issues I should know about." I stood.

"I'll do that." Officer Purdue stood as well. He held out his hand and I shook it. "Take care of yourself, Krissy."

"You too," I said. "Be safe."

As I left the station, I debated whether or not I wanted to go home or back to the office. The responsible side of me won out and I headed to Mirage, though I did make a pit stop first. There was something I needed to get first. When I arrived at work, unsurprisingly, DeVon wasn't there. I gave Tracy a smile when I passed and then retreated to my office to work on drafting

Mirage's official press release regarding Landon's coming out article. We had to maintain the perfect balance of supportive without seeming like we were exploiting his decision.

It took me a while to get focused, but once I did, I was able to work straight through until it was time to go home. As I saved the file, I was at least satisfied that I'd accomplished something good today. The press release was probably the best thing I'd ever written because I'd gone over every individual word half a dozen times to make sure it was perfect.

As I drove home, however, thoughts of Landon and the press release slipped away and all I could think about was how things were going to play out with DeVon when he got home. There was a lot we needed to talk about, not the least of which was what was going on with him. The restlessness I'd felt before returned when I saw that he wasn't already there. Not a surprise since he'd been coming home late every night since we'd gotten back from New York, but it didn't irritate me any less, especially considering the circumstances. Of course, since I was irritated, I didn't want to eat and that made me queasy again, which, in turn, turned irritation into annoyance. By the time the front door opened and DeVon walked in, I was well into frustrated and heading straight towards pissed. Still, I kept myself calm. DeVon and I were both passionate enough people that things could get intense if we didn't keep ourselves in check.

"You're still up." He looked tired.

"I am," I leaned against the arm of the chair. "And you're home late."

"I am," he repeated. He tossed his keys onto the kitchen table. "I already ate dinner so I hope you didn't hold it for me."

"No," I said tersely. "I didn't. I just feel like I haven't seen you since we got back from New York."

"I've been working." He pulled a beer out of the refrigerator. "We were gone for a few days, and then you were sick."

My mouth flattened into a line. He was seriously going to throw that in my face? Especially now? "Seems like you've been doing a lot of out-of-office work."

His face took on that blank expression I hated so much. "A lot of field work lately."

I made a non-committal noise and continued, "I asked Melissa, but she said she wasn't sure where you were going."

"You asked Melissa about what I was doing?" His eyes flashed.

"Well, considering you haven't been around to ask, I had to go somewhere." I could hear an edge wanting to come into my voice. I held up a hand and took a moment to calm myself. "You weren't at the office today. What were you working on?"

He took a long drink of his beer and looked over my head. "I've been trying to get something on Garrison Mayflower to fix this whole Landon situation."

I wasn't sure if it was the direct lie to my face that did it or the fact that he obviously hadn't been paying attention to anything I'd been saying for the past week, but I snapped.

"Bullshit!"

His eyes flicked down to my face and they were flat, expressionless.

I marched over to him and poked him in the chest with my finger. "That is such a fucking load of bullshit! The Landon 'situation' has been resolved. And if you'd been around or listened to me, you'd know that. The fact that you can't even come up with a fucking decent lie..." My voice trailed off. "You know what, I feel like shit and I'm not going to do this now. I'm going to bed. Sleep in the fucking guest room because I don't want you anywhere near me."

I turned to stomp off when he said something that turned my blood to ice.

"It's my fucking bedroom."

"Fine." I didn't turn to look at him, unsure if I'd start crying or slap him. I wanted to do both. "I'll sleep in the guest room. I suppose that's appropriate since that's where you generally make your women sleep, right?"

The tears were burning at my eyelids and I hurried off before they could spill over. I could barely swallow around the lump in my throat as I slammed the door behind me. I sank to the floor and buried my face in my hands, bursting into tears for the second time in two days. I sat there for an hour and he never came to see if I was okay. Something had broken between us and I didn't know what it was or why it had happened, only that if we didn't fix it, soon we wouldn't be able to. And I couldn't bear to think about what would happen if I lost DeVon now.

# FOURTEEN
## DEVON

The moment I saw that Krissy was still awake, I knew I was fucked. The past week, she'd been wrapped up in the whole Landon thing and not feeling well, so I'd been able to avoid the issue as I tried to figure out what I wanted to do. I'd always intended to tell her, but things had gotten more complicated today after I met Emmett.

I'd been thinking about him and the ultimatum Sasha had set when I'd walked into the house and seen that the shit was about to hit the fan. I'd tried to be vague, hoping Krissy would accept my flimsy excuses, but I hadn't been surprised that hadn't worked. Then she'd asked specifically about today and the first thing that had popped into my head had been to act like I had been trying to help her with the Landon issue.

She'd exploded and I knew I'd royally fucked myself when she made it perfectly clear that she hadn't been fooled at all by my claims of 'working late.' Then she'd told me to sleep in the guest room and I'd said the stupidest thing to ever come out of my mouth. I didn't even know why I said it, only that it had been something that the old me would've said. The me I'd been before I'd fallen in love. The one who'd been with Sasha and hundreds of other women. Since Krissy had moved in, I'd never really thought about the house as 'mine' but 'ours.' Everything had become 'ours.'

As she slammed the guest room door, I let out a stream of curses in English and Italian, and slammed my hand down on the counter. What the hell had I been thinking? I drained the rest of my beer and then started looking through the cabinets for something stronger. Had I subconsciously been trying to sabotage what Krissy and I had so I wouldn't need to make a decision?

My thoughts involuntarily went back to earlier today when I'd met Sasha and Emmett in Pan Pacific Park. She'd been overly friendly and flirtatious, but I'd kept my distance, hoping to make it clear that I wasn't interested in her, just Emmett.

He was a sweet boy. Tall for his age, with thick black hair and green eyes. I couldn't really see myself or Sasha in him, but neither Franco nor I had looked more like one parent than the other. The timeline was accurate, so unless Sasha was lying about her lovers around that same period, Emmett was my son. I hadn't introduced myself as his father, though. I wanted to talk to him a bit first, get a feel for how he'd take the news.

We'd had a good conversation, but Sasha had kept butting in, making comments here and there about how the three of us were going to be a family. She'd also started to hang on me, wrapping her arm around mine, like we were some sort of couple in the park with our son. When I'd finally untangled myself from her and taken a step back, I'd seen a glimpse of unstable Sasha again. She'd sent Emmett off to play again and told me we'd needed to talk.

She'd laid it out for me then and I'd seen that she hadn't come back to get money from me. She and Emmett were a package deal. I didn't get to have a relationship with him and not have one with her...on her terms. She didn't want to be amicable exes or even friends. She wanted me back as a lover and, in the very near future, a husband. We three would be a family.

I'd told her that I was in love with someone else, that Krissy was the only person I wanted in my life and that she and I had been together for almost a year. Sasha hadn't been happy with that, but she'd stayed in control. She'd made it simple at that point. I would have to choose between Emmett and Krissy. If I didn't give Krissy up, I wouldn't be allowed to be a part of my son's life.

I'd automatically countered with a legal dispute. I had the money to do it and I knew she didn't. I'd told her that I'd get a DNA test to prove paternity and then sue for full custody. I'd reminded her that I had friends in high places and she'd be lucky if she managed to get joint custody.

The real Sasha, the one that hid behind the pretty face and smile, had come out then. She'd told me that if I went anywhere near a lawyer or courtroom, she'd take Emmett and run. I'd never see my son again. Even though I didn't know the boy that well and I didn't have the scientific proof that he was mine, I couldn't, in all good conscience, leave a child with someone like Sasha. Who knew what kind of damage she'd inflicted on him already.

That meant I was faced with an impossible choice. Abandon my son to his psychotic mother or lose the only woman I'd ever really loved. Both options tore at my heart and I didn't know what to do.

I couldn't not be a part of Emmett's life now that I knew about him. I'd never thought about having kids, not seriously anyway. Growing up, Franco had always been the one we'd all assumed would get married and have kids. He was a ladies' man – that ran in the family – but he had always loved kids and had never balked at the idea of getting married. I was the one who was supposed to spend my life hopping from woman to woman, never settling down. The one who'd be the eternal bachelor. Even when I'd gotten engaged to Haley, I'd never really been able to see myself as a husband. And I'd never even considered kids. Sure, she'd mentioned them from time to time and I'd never said no, but my heart hadn't ever been in it. It hit me, for the first time ever, that maybe Haley had known all along that a family wasn't in the cards for me. She could've found a better way to tell me, but I could see now how it would've been inevitable.

I had no idea how to be a parent, but I'd taught myself a lot over the years, and I could learn how to do this, too. I'd been fortunate enough to grow up with a great father, and I'd known too many men who were horrible ones. I couldn't be anything less than the kind of man my father had raised me to be.

But to be that man, to be a father to Emmett, I'd have to let go of the person who made me a better man. The thought of losing Krissy was the most excruciating thing I'd experienced since the death of my mother, and I knew that if it hurt this badly just to consider it, the actual action would be so much worse.

I found the tequila tucked away in a back corner and drank a quarter of it in one gulp. It burned and I almost coughed. I took another swig and then headed for the bedroom. Our bedroom. My bedroom. I looked at the closed guest room door as I passed but didn't stop. I couldn't tell her tonight. I didn't know how I'd ever tell her. How do you tell someone that you love them more than your own life, but that you have to give them up because it's the right thing to do?

I sat down on the edge of my bed and buried my head in my hands. Usually, when I was upset, I got angry, but I couldn't manage anger this time. All that wanted to come were tears and, for the first time in a very long time, I let myself cry. I cried for the future I had never known I wanted and would now never have. I cried because I knew I could never be as good of a father as the one I'd had, but that I was all Emmett had. Mostly, though, I cried because I'd hurt the woman I loved, and I was only going to hurt her more before this was all over.

## FIFTEEN
## KRISSY

I spent too much of that night crouched over the toilet off of the guest room, dry heaving since there was nothing left in my stomach to come up. I desperately wanted the comfort and safety of my room. My bathroom. I wanted to soak in my tub and wrap myself up in my robe. I wanted to sleep in my own bed. But most of all, I wanted it to be mine. My home that I had made with the man I loved, and I was afraid that I was never going to have that again. If I'd ever had it in the first place.

I got maybe three hours' sleep in all and I found myself wondering if DeVon'd had as rough a night as I had, or if he'd just slept straight through after emptying his head of whatever it was he'd been dwelling on all week. One thing I did know, he hadn't been throwing up all night and half the morning.

I heard him walk by at about five thirty but I didn't go out to him. He didn't stop, so I supposed he didn't want to talk to me, either. Except I did want to talk to him. I wanted to know why he'd said those horrible things. Why he was being so cold and distant. I wanted to know what had happened this week that had changed everything. Or had it been changing for a while and I just hadn't noticed?

Finally, by about seven, I was tired of all the wondering, all of the conjecturing. I needed to have this done and over with. I couldn't handle another day like this. Not now. I showered and dressed. Like I normally did when I wasn't feeling well, I chose every garment carefully, applied my make-up and did my hair. When I finished, I looked in the mirror. If I hadn't known how pale I was or about the bags under my eyes that my make-up was hiding, I would've thought I was just going in for another day of work.

I'd chosen one of my favorite summer dresses, a cute pale green that was business casual with just a hint of sexy. Underneath, I was wearing the lingerie that Landon and I had chosen. It was sheer white lace that barely left anything to the imagination. It didn't really make me feel better physically, but it did wonders for my own well-being.

As I took the elevator up, I let myself feel all of the anger and frustration of the past week, let it give me the strength that Landon had said DeVon loved about me. I thought back on the other times I'd barged into his office, temper flaring, to confront him about something he'd done or said. Sometimes it had been a misunderstanding on my part. Other times, he'd done something worth my ire. In a matter of minutes, I'd know which it was this time.

Melissa looked up when I stepped off the elevator, but she didn't say anything, either to tell me not to go in or to encourage me to keep going. I gave her a nod of acknowledgement and then walked in.

DeVon looked up and I almost faltered. He looked worse than I did, and considering the amount of time I'd spent in the bathroom, that was saying something. His hair was a mess, his face pale, and the bags under his eyes bigger than the ones under mine. I hadn't noticed last night, but he looked like he'd lost weight, too. His clothes were rumpled and looked like he'd either slept in them or had picked them up off the floor. He didn't look surprised to see me, but he didn't look glad, either.

"Krissy." He leaned back in his chair, his shoulders slumped.

I continued over to the desk, expecting him to come over and give me a kiss, but he didn't. I put my fingertips on the desk, using it to keep me steady.

"We need to talk."

A resigned expression passed over his face, mixed with something that looked like pain. I waited for him to start, but he didn't.

"Ever since we got back from New York, you've been acting weird. And then last night..." I paused, a pang going through me as I remembered what he'd said to me.

"Look," DeVon said. He pinched the bridge of his nose. "I'm sorry, Krissy. I shouldn't have said that last night. I was tired–"

"So was I!" I interrupted. My temper was starting to rise. How could he use being tired as an excuse to basically say that the place I'd been living for the past several months wasn't my home, that I was just a guest in his place? "I've been fucking sick and tired since we got back, but I'm not blowing off my responsibilities or treating you like a stranger. I'm not the one who said–"

"I have a son."

He said it quietly, but it was like an explosion had gone off. I stared at him, unsure I'd heard him correctly. "Say again?"

He sighed and pushed himself out of the chair. He walked around the desk so that we were only a few inches apart. He started to reach out to me and then stuffed his hands in his pockets.

"The day after we got back, a woman came into my office. I'd been with her about seven years ago. For a week." His words were flat and he wasn't looking at me. "I broke things off. She didn't take it well. I had to take out a restraining order."

Oh, fuck. This was worse than I'd thought.

"She came the other day and said that we had a son together. A six-year-old boy named Emmett."

The face of the boy from the park flashed in front of me, followed by the woman I'd seen flirting with DeVon. It all made sense. Her touching him. His tension, but not pushing her away.

"I didn't know." His eyes flicked up to mine and I saw the anguish in them now. "I didn't know."

My mind was spinning, and the lawyer in me caught up first. "And you're sure that she's telling the truth? That he's your son?" His head jerked up. "Did you get a DNA test?"

"I'm not stupid, Krissy," DeVon snapped. He raked his hand through his hair. He turned away. "She told me his birthday. Told me when her last sexual encounter had been before she'd been with me, and when she'd fucked someone after me. The time doesn't fit for anyone but me."

"But she could've lied," I pressed. "It's not like you'd be able to prove otherwise unless you get Emmett tested."

"She told me that she lied about being on the pill when we were together. And that she'd poked holes in the condoms we used because she wanted us to be together forever." DeVon's eyes were flashing. "I take care of my fucking responsibilities, Krissy!"

"But what if he's not yours?"

"That's what this is about, isn't it?" He took a step towards me. "You don't want him to be my son."

I stepped into him, my index finger a couple centimeters from his chest. "Don't you dare put this on me. I don't give a fuck if you have a son, a daughter or a whole fucking starting line-up! And don't act like you're so high and mighty. You're the one who's been lying to me for the past week. We're supposed to be partners, DeVon! In business and in life and you kept me in the dark!"

"Because I didn't know what to do!"

I blinked. I'd never heard that much anguish in DeVon's voice.

He reached up and cupped the side of my face. "She gave me an ultimatum, Krissy. I can't be a part of Emmett's life without being a part of hers."

My chest tightened. I had a feeling that wasn't all.

"And that means...I have to give you up." His voice broke. "It's you or my son."

I looked at him for a moment, the flurry of emotions inside me making it nearly impossible to think. And that was good because I didn't want to think. I didn't want to think about what DeVon had been carrying alone because he didn't want to hurt me. I didn't want to think about that poor boy being used as a pawn. And I certainly didn't want to think about the choice he had to make or what that choice would be. I already knew the answer.

I did the only thing I could do. I kissed him.

I felt his surprise, and then his tongue was pushing between my lips. I wrapped my arms around his neck and pressed my body against his, feeling his cock harden against my hip. One hand buried itself in my hair, yanking my head to the side as his mouth made its way down my neck, biting and sucking with an almost desperate haste.

His need fed my own and I ran my hands down his chest to the waistband of his pants. I didn't know what the future held, but I knew what I wanted now. The hand not currently buried in my hair ran down my back and up under the skirt of my dress. I moaned as his fingers caressed the back of my thigh and then slipped up to my ass. The heat of his palm radiated through the thin material.

"I need you." His voice was ragged as he lifted me onto the desk.

I let my hands do the talking as I opened his pants and reached inside. He grabbed my breast, squeezing as I wrapped my fingers around his now-hard cock. He released me as he pushed my dress up around my waist and I spread my legs.

"Babe?"

I knew what his question was and I nodded my answer. It was going to hurt. I was barely wet. But I knew the pain would fade and DeVon would make it worth every bit of it. He pulled aside the crotch of my panties and buried himself inside me with one quick snap of his hips.

I pressed my face against DeVon's chest and screamed, muffling the sound and those that followed as he fucked me. My body shook as each stroke stretched me fast and hard. His thumb rubbed my clit, sending waves of pleasure through me, turning pain into something so much deeper, more intense. I squeezed my eyes closed, my nails digging at his back and ass as he thrust into me with brutal, rapid strokes. The world was reduced to the joining of our bodies, the sound of my name being repeated over and over again.

Then my world exploded in a burst of white light and I clung to him, riding the waves of pleasure even as he continued to thrust into me. His hands tightened around me as he groaned, emptying himself inside me.

"I love you," he breathed into my ear. "I love you so much."

"I love you, too." I raised my head and met his eyes. I reached up and brushed back his hair. "And we'll figure this out. I'm not going anywhere."

He kissed me then, our bodies still joined. I meant what I'd said. I wasn't going anywhere. I just didn't add that I was going to find out the truth about Sasha and Emmett. One way or another.

## SIXTEEN

## KRISSY

We didn't talk about Sasha or Emmett or the choice DeVon had to make. We talked about work and what Landon had done. I told DeVon everything that had happened between Mayflower and me, including his offer and what I'd almost done. He hadn't wasted time or energy being angry. He was enough like me that he understood my reasons. We had a conference call with Landon, as much to reassure him that we were okay as to touch base about his interview. I wasn't entirely sure we were okay, but our friend didn't need anything else to worry about.

I didn't go back to my office the rest of the day and DeVon didn't question it. We worked mostly in silence, going through files and reading scripts. We sat on the couch, leaning against each other as if we were working from home. Lunch was ordered in and Melissa told us that DeVon's three o'clock meeting with Steven Morrison had been rescheduled. She didn't say it, but I suspected she'd been the one who'd done the rescheduling, not Steven. The expression on her face told me that she suspected something wasn't quite right, but she was too much of a professional to ask.

We left on time, picking up some take-out on the way to the

penthouse, even though I suspected DeVon had as little appetite as I did. The nausea I'd been feeling since getting back from New York was gone, but in its place was that gnawing emptiness that came with receiving a huge shock.

We didn't make love that night, but we did spend hours soaking in our massive bathtub, holding each other until the water started to get cold. Then we went to bed and held each other there, neither one of us wanting to consider that we might have spent our last day together. I didn't know who fell asleep first, or when it happened, only that when I opened my eyes, my pillow was wet from tears and DeVon was gone.

A piece of paper rested on his pillow. I stared at it, willing it to disappear, praying that yesterday had been a bad dream. That everything that had happened since coming home had just been the product of airplane food and jet-lag. When nothing changed, I reached for the note. Pretending it wasn't there wouldn't change the message. I braced myself to have my heart torn out, and then opened it.

Krissy, I'm sure you looked at this with more than a little trepidation, believing that I had taken the coward's way out, unable to face you as I broke both our hearts. Nothing could be further from the truth.

My heart gave a wild leap and I tried not to hope as I kept reading.

I've been awake for a few hours, watching you sleep and trying to imagine giving you up. I can't do it. To lose you would be to lose the best part of me, and what sort of father could I be without that part? Sasha wants to hurt me because I hurt her. She wants me to choose her, and I can't do that. I'm going to see her and I'm going to do whatever it takes to convince her that I can't lose you. I'm hoping that she'll be satisfied to see me begging, to see herself as the one in control, the one with the power. If that doesn't work, I'll ask her to name her price. She's said she doesn't want the money, only for Emmett and the two of us to be a family, but I'm hoping that, when given the chance, she'll take what she can get. If it means giving up Mirage and working in some factory, barely making ends meet, I'll do it. I would hate to ask you to live like that, but if it's the only way we can be together and I can see my son, I hope you would understand. More likely, she would ask for cash and come back every so often, threatening to take Emmett if she wasn't given more, but that is a price I am willing to pay. You are the only price too costly. If she refuses, we will figure out another way, you and I, because we are part-ners. I love you.

I read the last two sentences again.

He'd chosen me.

Tears burned my eyes and I took a slow breath, looking up at the ceiling as I tried to blink them back.

He wasn't giving up. That, I thought, was what had scared me the most about this whole thing. DeVon was a fighter. I'd known that from moment one and it had been one of the things about him that had both attracted and annoyed me. It was also what made him so good at his job. Soft people couldn't succeed in this business. There had to be a fire, a fight inside that refused to give up. When he'd told me the choice Sasha had given him, he'd sounded resigned, as if there was nothing he could do. Now that I knew he wasn't going to just do what Sasha wanted, relief flooded through me. I hadn't been willing to admit how much the thought of losing him terrified me.

I looked at the clock, surprised when I saw that it was mid-morning. I hadn't slept that late in a long time, not unless I was sick. I didn't know what time DeVon had left, but I was sure his conversation with Sasha wouldn't be a short one. From the little he'd told me, she didn't seem like the most stable and under-standing of people. I had some dysfunctional people in my family, not the least of which was my narcissistic mother, but Sasha sounded like she was worse.

I couldn't pace around here, waiting for DeVon to call or show up. We hadn't been staying here much, spending most of our time in our house, so there wasn't really any tidying up to do. The cleaning crew would've come through on Thursday, and nothing had accumulated since then. I'd never be able to concentrate on a book or movie, even if I had felt like trying. I could leave a note and head out to the house, but I didn't think that would be any better. The cleaning crew would've been through there yesterday while DeVon and I had been at work, so there wouldn't be any busy work for me to do, and I was far too distracted to try anything else.

For the first time in a long time, I wished I was back in New York. I didn't want to be there because I liked it better than LA or because I didn't feel like this was home. In fact, it wasn't really New York I wanted. It was Carrie. I want to be able to go to my friend's place, curl up on the couch with her and pour out everything I was feeling while we waited for Dena and Leslie to come over. I had friends here, but none who I really felt comfortable sharing any of this with. Melissa and Tracy both worked here and I tried very hard not to bring up things about DeVon and my relationship with them. I would talk to Landon about things like that, but he'd had his interview yesterday and I didn't think he needed anything else to worry about.

I sighed. There was one place I could go where I wouldn't have to worry about anyone asking questions and where the environment might make it easier to concentrate. It was stifling hot outside, despite noon being a couple hours away, so I chose a white sundress with little rosebuds. It wasn't quite right for a normal work day, but it would be fine for today. I wanted something bright and cheery. I firmly believed that the way a person dressed could affect the mood they were in as well as the one they projected. It was one of the reasons I often dressed up when I felt like shit.

It was about ten-thirty when I hailed a cab and had it take me to Mirage. I could've called one of the town cars, but I didn't want to call one, have it drop me off and then have to call it back a couple hours later because DeVon was at the apartment. I'd left him a note saying where I was and explaining that I hadn't called him because I hadn't wanted to interrupt if he was in the middle of something. I also didn't want to run the risk of Sasha seeing who was calling and that setting her off.

When I got to Mirage, the only people there were the two security guards on the early weekend shift and they both smiled and nodded as I walked by. While DeVon and I didn't make a habit of working on weekends, it wasn't a strange enough occurrence that anyone would think it was weird.

I spent the next twenty minutes or so surfing the web, scouring sites for any sign of Mayflower's pictures or any hints that Landon's story had leaked. All I found was a teaser from Proud and Out saying that they had an exclusive in their Monday edition in which a huge star would be coming out. I was glad Landon didn't have to wait long for it to be out there. I knew that he was like me. The waiting was the worst part. The two of us were 'rip off the band-aid' kind of people. He'd want to get it done and over with so he could move on with his life.

I was thinking through logistics for Monday when my cell rang. My heart started to race, then fell when I saw that it wasn't DeVon. It was, however, the precinct number. I'd forgotten that I'd dropped off a picture of Sasha before I'd known who she was or what she wanted. It was probably just repeat information, but I answered it anyway. I didn't want Officer Purdue to think I was blowing him off.

"Hello," I answered.

"Ms. Jensen."

My eyebrows went up. That was formal cop voice, not friendly cop voice.

"This is Officer Purdue."

"Yes?"

"I ran that picture you gave me and got a name. Stacy Richards."

I sat up straighter. In Hollywood, aliases and stage names weren't uncommon, but my gut told me that Sasha hadn't been trying out for a local play when she'd used that name.

"The police in Minnesota are actually looking for her. I assume you took that picture locally?"

"What do they want her for?" I asked.

"Questioning in an on-going investigation." Officer Purdue was intentionally vague. He'd chosen his words carefully, reminding me that the police weren't supposed to comment about on-going investigations. "Do you know where she is?"

"I took the picture at Pan Pacific Park," I said. "Two days ago."

Officer Purdue swore, confirming my suspicion that Sasha didn't have overdue parking tickets. "Do you know where she is?"

"No," I said honestly. "But I do have some information about her and may be able to find where she's at." My mind was racing, trying to figure out the best way to do this. "Is she a person of interest or an official suspect for something?"

He sighed. "I know better than to try to talk you into giving me the info, so how about we just cut to the chase. I'll fax you the file I have and you tell me what you know."

"Agreed." I gave him my office fax number and, a few minutes later, two papers came through. As I picked them up, I gave the first part of the information I had. "She's going by Sasha Richmond here. I think that's her real name because she used it when she was here before."

"She's from LA?"

"I don't know," I said as I began to skim the papers. "But she was here about seven years ago, using the same name. She'll have a restraining order under that name."

"A restraining order?" Something shifted in his tone, telling me that bit of news might be related to the charges in Minnesota.

I figured I might as well tell him now. He'd see it when he ran her name and then he'd be pissed I hadn't told him personally. "It's from DeVon. He used to...date her and she didn't take it well when he dumped her."

Officer Purdue let out a very unprofessional stream of expletives that would've made me worried if I hadn't been joining him as I read the charge.

Kidnapping.

Sasha was a person of interest in the kidnapping of a little boy nearly three years ago. A three-year-old boy...with black hair and green eyes.

I sank down in my seat, fighting the urge to be sick.

"You're telling me that this woman is your boyfriend's ex?" Officer Purdue was practically shouting in the phone.

"Was it a custody issue?" I asked faintly. My head was spinning.

"What?"

"The boy. Is Sasha the prime suspect because she's the boy's biological mother and she'd changed her mind about an adoption?" It sounded far-fetched, but I knew it was a possibility. And I needed to know if that chance was there. Because, if it wasn't, that changed everything.

"No," Officer Purdue said. "The boy's biological parents are in St. Paul, thinking they'll never see their son again. Stacy Richards or Sasha Richmond, whatever her name is, had been the boy's nanny for two years and then disappeared the same day he did."

"Fuck." The word was barely a whisper.

"What?"

I closed my eyes, unsure if I felt relief or horror. Relief that DeVon wasn't going to have to choose. Horror over who that little boy really was.

"She's here with a boy she says is DeVon's son. He's six years old and I'm nearly positive he's the boy in that picture."

I'd put Sasha and Emmett up at the Hilton when I'd seen the flea-bag motel where they'd been staying. It had been the one Sasha had insisted on when I'd said I'd be moving them and I knew it was because we'd had a couple trysts here during the week we'd been together. I didn't go into any of that, though. The Hilton had an excellent reputation for protecting the privacy of its guests and once I'd told them that the only person they were allowed to share information with was Krissy, I knew I didn't have to worry about the press finding out.

I had to admit, I was actually a little surprised that Sasha hadn't threatened to do that. She'd flaunted our relationship to the press before, thriving in the spotlight. I would've thought she'd want pictures of the three of us together, my secret little family. Krissy and my relationship hadn't really been a big story, especially once the media had realized that we didn't air our dirty laundry, but a scandal always made things more interesting.

I was still mulling that over when I got to their room. I had a key, but I didn't intend to use it. I wanted to make it perfectly clear from the beginning that I wasn't the missing piece in their puzzle. I wanted to get to know Emmett, but Sasha wasn't going to be part of the package.

"DeVon!" She threw her arms around me as soon as she opened the door. "You came!"

I quickly disentangled her arms and stepped into the room. "We need to talk."

"Of course," she said.

I watched as she shifted into her serious face. I hadn't realized it when we'd been together before, but her facial expressions looked more like how she thought they were supposed to look rather than how she actually felt. It wasn't a surprise I hadn't realized it before. The only time I'd really cared about the expressions on her face had been when we'd been fucking, and now I wondered if those had even been genuine.

"There are a lot of things we need to discuss." She sounded like a child trying to be an adult. "Logistics. Do we move in together right away or will that be too confusing for Emmett? Should we get engaged first so that he realizes this is forever? I don't want him thinking—"

"Sasha, stop!" The words came out more harshly than I'd intended, but I couldn't help myself. She was further gone than I'd thought. I couldn't leave Emmett with her. No matter what it cost, I had to get him away from her.

She gave me a hurt look, but I could see the anger glinting in her eyes.

"Where's Emmett?" I looked around, not wanting him to hear any of this. He didn't need to know that his mother was trying to blackmail me. She may have been crazy, but I wasn't going to be the kind of man who bad-mouthed his kid's mother anywhere the kid could hear it.

"He's taking a nap," she said.

I frowned. I didn't know a lot about kids but something seemed off that a six-year-old was taking a nap at nearly ten in the morning. I didn't ask about it, though. I had enough on my plate at the moment. I filed that away for later.

"Let's sit down." I gestured towards the love-seat. I would've preferred not to sit so close to her, but I didn't think she'd take kindly to me sitting in one of the chairs as if I was purposefully putting distance between us, and I needed her in a better mood.

"I know this has been hard for you," I began. "Raising Emmett on your own." She nodded, giving me those wide eyes that I was sure had melted many a man's heart over the years. "Especially financially."

"The sacrifice was worth it."

Somehow, she made a statement that should have sounded noble and motherly seem like it had come out of some sort of poorly acted play. I wondered if she'd always been like this and I just hadn't noticed or if I was more aware of what was genuine and what was not since I'd been with Krissy.

"I was wondering." I chose my words carefully, knowing that the wrong word could ruin everything. "Since you haven't had any time to yourself in six years, if, instead of staying here with me and Emmett, you'd prefer to go out, go someplace exciting and fun. All expenses paid, of course." The corners of her mouth tightened. "Or, if you'd rather stay here, I'd be more than happy to pay for an apartment or a house, whichever you'd prefer."

"You don't want to be with me." The statement came out flat.

"Sasha, I'm sorry. It's too late for us." I didn't add that I never would've stayed with her in the first place because she was nuttier than a Christmas fruitcake. That would've been counter-productive.

"Because of her." She snarled the word. "That woman you're with."

"I love her, Sasha." I tried to say it as gently as possible.

"Bullshit," she hissed. "You don't love anyone."

I started to be offended, but then realized that she was right. At least, the person she'd known all those years ago, he hadn't been capable of love. I couldn't tell her that Krissy was the one who'd made the difference.

"Let me provide for you and Emmett." I tried a different tact. "Whatever you need. Whatever you want. I'll write you a check for a hundred thousand dollars right now."

"That's all he's worth to you?" she asked.

My fingers dug into my legs as I struggled to keep my temper. "I just picked a random number. Half a million for what I missed and then that same amount every year on top of expenses."

"You think half a million dollars will make up for the birthdays you missed?"

I wanted to point out that it was her fault I'd missed six years. Instead, I asked, "How much?"

She pretended to think for a moment. "Five million."

I nodded. I'd have to shuffle some assets, but that would far from break me.

"To start with."

I tried not to glare. I'd meant what I'd told Krissy, that I'd give it all up. I just hated how Sasha was manipulating things.

She leaned against me. "Five million could buy you a lot of pussy." She ran her hand up my leg until she was way too close to my crotch. "If I take enough money, will Krissy leave you?" She slipped the strap of her tank top off of her shoulder. "Come on, DeVon. Don't you remember all of the fun we had together?"

I closed my eyes, hoping that if I didn't respond, she'd take the hint. If I had to push her away, things were going to go very badly.

"No other man has been able to get me off like you did. And

I'll bet your little girlfriend doesn't let you have as much fun as I did. Does she let you whip her? I want you to whip me. I'll bet you want it, too. I still have my clit pierced. I think about you when I play with it. Would she get pierced for you? Let you spank her so hard her ass is bruised for a week? I will. I'll let you fuck me until I scream. Tie me up." She picked up my hand and put it on her neck. "I'll let you squeeze–"

"No." I didn't move her, but I did move myself. I stood up and she almost fell over. "I don't want you, Sasha. Not anymore."

She stood, not bothering to pull up her strap even when it fell low enough to reveal a sliver of a toffee-colored nipple. "Get out!"

"Emmett–" I started to say.

"Get the hell out!" She practically screamed. "We're leaving and you're never going to see your son again!"

I backed out of the room, not knowing what else to do. If she caused a big enough scene, security would be called, and then the cops. I didn't want Emmett to see that. As the door closed, a pain went through me. I'd lost him. I hadn't even known it until just now how much I wanted him, and he was gone. There was no way Sasha was going to let me be a part of his life. Not now.

My chest hurt and I could hardly breathe as I walked down the hallway towards the elevator. What was I going to do? I couldn't just let them leave, but I didn't have any legal grounds to stand on. By the time I could get a court order for a paternity test, no matter how good a lawyer I hired, she'd be gone. I could hire a PI to find her, but if my name wasn't on the birth certificate, I'd still need that test before I could do anything. And that was if a judge believed me when I said I hadn't known about Emmett. All Sasha had to do was claim she'd told me and I hadn't paid child support in six years. If she started in on our sex life, I'd be lucky if the courts didn't bar me from seeing him.

I wandered out of the lobby and sat on one of the benches. The sun beat down overhead and the air was thick, but I barely registered any of it. All I could think about was how I was going to fix this. I had to be able to fix it. I'd made a great life for myself here, made something of myself by working hard and never quitting.

The only way I could think of was the one thing I didn't want to do. I pressed my hand against my chest but the pain there wasn't physical. Could I ask Krissy to step back, to take a break until I could spent enough time with Emmett to get proof of paternity and then sue for custody? Would she be willing to do that for however long it took? Could I do it? If it was just a couple months, I thought I could, but deep down I knew that it would never be over with Sasha. Every time Emmett would be with her, I'd be worrying that she'd run with him. I could have all of the papers in the world saying he was mine, but once she had him, if she thought for a moment that Krissy and I were together, I had no doubt she'd bolt.

I buried my head in my hands. What was I going to do?

In my pocket, my phone buzzed, but I let it go. Whoever it was, they could wait. I was in no state to deal with anything else today. Nothing else could be as important as this.

# EIGHTEEN
## KRISSY

"Dammit, DeVon! Pick up your fucking phone!" I was glad there wasn't anyone in the office to hear me. I'd tried calling him twice with the same result. Ringing until it finally went to voicemail. The first time, I left a message for him to call me back, and then I'd called again. I supposed it was possible he was in the middle of talking to Sasha, but that didn't make me feel any better.

I'd finished reading the file Officer Purdue had sent over and it was worse than I'd originally thought. From what I'd gathered, Sasha had claimed to be someone named Stacy Richards and had gotten a job as a nanny to little Joey Turner. She'd been quiet and had always done things well, but after Joey and she both disappeared, everyone seemed to remember that they'd always thought she was a bit off. That hadn't been the part that had freaked me out, however. That was about what they'd found when they'd gone into the room she'd been using.

She'd had dozens of books and pamphlets about having a baby. She'd gone through, highlighting various passages and writing dates next to some things. Joey's mom had said that the dates had been times when Joey had done the things that were highlighted. His first steps. Cutting his first tooth. And some of the things had happened before she'd been hired. That wouldn't have even been too weird – maybe just a bit obsessive – except she had pictures from some of those events. Pictures that weren't ones she'd gotten out of the family's album. That would've been bad enough. These, however, were ones that looked like someone had taken them from a distance. I'd dealt with enough PIs investigating cheating spouses to recognize long-lens shots.

I had no doubt now that Emmett was Joey Turner. The only other option was too horrible to think about. That Joey Turner was long-dead and Emmett was some other kid she'd snatched. It wasn't only DeVon I was worried about. If Emmett was Joey, she'd had that poor kid for three years. Did he even know he wasn't her son? What would it be like for him when he found out the truth?

I cursed again and kicked the desk for good measure. All I got out of that was an aching toe, but the pain did help clear my head. I knew the cops were looking now, but I'd forgotten to tell them that DeVon was with Sasha right now. That was an angle I knew of but they didn't, and I had a pretty good idea of how to find DeVon and Sasha. It was nice to know my skills as a former divorce lawyer were going to do some good. I'd tracked down more than one unfaithful husband during my time at Webster and Steinberg.

I was going to start with some of the cheaper hotels, but as soon as I picked up the phone to make the call, I realized that there was no way DeVon would let someone he thought was his son stay in even a modest three-star hotel. I also had a good idea that Sasha wasn't the kind of woman who'd take anything less than four stars.

I called two five-star hotels that DeVon and I had been to, but there weren't any charges under his name. It had taken a bit of wheedling to get the information out of them, but the lawyer in me had eventually won out. When I called the Hilton, I prepared myself for another argument, but it didn't come.

"Hi, my name is Krissy Jensen from Mirage Talent, and I'm calling about someone who may be a guest at your establishment." I kept my voice bright and professional. If they heard desperation, they'd be less likely to help me, thinking I was a stalker or jealous ex or something like that. The irony was, that's who I was trying to protect DeVon from.

"How may I help you, Ms. Jensen?" The woman who answered the phone had a cool, pleasant voice.

"I need to know if you have any rooms charged to DeVon Ricci. It may be under Mirage Talent." I didn't think it would be, but I was hoping she'd think I was calling as an employee checking up on reservations rather than a girlfriend trying to find her man, albeit not for the reasons she suspected.

"Just a moment, please."

I heard the tapping that indicated she was looking for something on her computer, and then she came back. "You understand, Ms. Jensen, that under normal circumstances, it would be entirely inappropriate for me to hand out information about our guests, that we respect their privacy."

I started to reply, but she was still talking.

"However, a special note was placed on this account. We were told that we could reveal information to you alone."

"So you're saying there is a room under DeVon's name?"

"I'm saying that should you come to the hotel with a photograph ID, I would be able to provide you with the information I do have."

"I'll be there in ten minutes." I hung up without waiting for a response and started to put my phone in my purse. "Dammit," I muttered. I wanted to find DeVon first so he didn't have to hear the truth from someone other than me, but I wasn't stupid enough to think that Sasha was going to just admit what she'd done and give up without a fight.

I waited until I was in the cab and halfway to the hotel before calling Officer Purdue back and telling him about the room. I didn't let him question me about where I was because I didn't want to lie and I knew for sure he'd tell me to stay away. It seemed more prudent to ask for forgiveness rather than permission at this point.

As the taxi grew closer to the hotel, I realized that I hadn't even considered what it was I was going to say. I couldn't very well just walk up and say, 'Hey, by the way, Sasha's a psycho who kidnapped some kid from Minnesota and brought him here to pretend that he was your son.' Somehow, I doubted that'd be the most tactful way to approach things. This was going to be hard enough for him to hear.

I tossed a few bills at the driver and headed for the front of the hotel. I was so focused on what I had to say that I almost walked right by him.

"DeVon!"

His head jerked up at the sound of my voice and the pain in his eyes made me wince. He stood, pulling me into a hug tight enough to drive the air from my lungs. He buried his face against the side of my neck. "I love you. I love you so much."

Anger rose inside me, anger at Sasha for making DeVon hurt like that, for lying to him. For her sake, I hoped the cops would arrive soon, because if I saw her, I wasn't sure I'd be able to keep from breaking her nose.

"I love you, too." I ran my hand over his hair.

"I don't want to lose you, but I can't abandon him, Krissy. I can't be selfish enough to keep you and give up my son."

I couldn't stand him thinking this way a moment longer. I hated how blunt I was going to be, but I couldn't think of another way to say it. "He's not your son."

DeVon stiffened but I didn't let him go. He had to hear it all.

"Sasha's lying. She's wanted in Minnesota. She kidnapped a toddler named Joey Turner three years ago."

I let him go this time when he pulled back. I pushed his hair away from his face.

"What are you saying, Krissy?"

I repeated myself, keeping it simple and clear because I knew this had to be hard to hear. "Emmett isn't your son."

"He's not my son." There were so many different emotions in that statement that I couldn't sort them out. He put his hand on my cheek. "I don't have to choose?"

My heart skipped a beat at the hope and relief in that question. "No, DeVon. You don't have to choose."

He lowered his head and kissed me, his mouth firm against mine. I could feel it now, just how much this had been hurting him, the desperation he'd felt, knowing how badly he would hurt me. I nipped at his bottom lip, then whispered against his mouth. "I love you."

It wasn't over yet, but we were together, and that was what mattered.

When Sasha had come to me and told me that I had a son, I'd thought my world had been turned upside-down, that everything had changed and nothing would ever be the same. Then I'd started to adjust to the idea of being a father and Sasha had given me the ultimatum and I couldn't imagine having to make that choice. I'd spent the last two weeks having my heart torn apart, and then Krissy had just unraveled everything with one simple statement.

Emmett wasn't my son.

I didn't have a son.

I didn't have to choose between him and Krissy.

I knew there was a lot we had to talk about and deal with, but there was something I had to do first.

The feel of her lips beneath mine was something I hadn't thought I would get to feel again. I'd been at that point, ready to give her up for the greater good, to never be with her, never touch her, all to do what was right. I knew it couldn't be a long kiss, but I made it a good one.

I moaned when her teeth closed on my bottom lip and I

wanted nothing more than to take her inside, rent a room and spend the rest of the weekend showing her how much I loved her and how sorry I was that she'd gone through this.

"I love you."

Not too long ago, I'd never imagined that I would want a woman to say those things to me, but now, I could hear those three words from her over and over again, and never grow tired of them.

I pushed her hair back from her face and sighed. "I intend to show you exactly how I feel about you, but first..."

"We need to make sure the boy's okay."

I nodded. "Have you called the police?" I asked.

"They should be about ten minutes behind me," she said, glancing back as if she'd be able to see them already. A worried look crossed her face. "If Sasha hears them coming, will she do something to Emmett – I mean, Joey?"

I thought of the look in Sasha's eyes when she'd told me to get out. She'd been crazy enough to kidnap a kid, hold him for three years and then try to convince me that he was mine. Who knew how many other men she'd tried this with. I wondered if there had been others before me. Men out there who thought they were looking for their son.

"She might," I said. I looked down at her. "He might not be my son, but he is in trouble. I can't let her take him."

"What can we do?"

A surge of love went through me as I saw the strength inside her come out. Her strength had been the first thing that had drawn me to her. Well, if I was completely honest, it was her incredibly hot body, but the strength had been there. She had so much spirit and fire, but that wasn't what I needed from her now. We couldn't stop Sasha with force or violence. Despite the fact that the idea of hurting a woman sickened me, it wouldn't do anyone any good.

I had something else in mind. And Krissy wasn't going to like it.

By the time I'd finished telling her my plan, I knew she didn't just dislike it. She loathed it, but she knew it was the right thing to do. So she stayed in front of the hotel to give the cops the room number while I went upstairs to distract Sasha.

I used the key this time because I wasn't sure if she'd let me in right away and I needed to get her away from the boy. If she was in a corner, I wasn't sure she wouldn't hurt him, just to spite everyone for thwarting her plans.

"What do you want?" she snapped from where she was sitting in the chair.

My eyes darted towards the boy. His eyes were wide and I could see the fear in them this time. I wanted to reassure him, tell him that it'd be okay and it would all be over soon, that he would be going back to his family, but there was nothing I could do or say with Sasha sitting right there, so I looked away from him and answered Sasha's question.

"It's over." I forced myself to think of the agony I would have felt if those words had been true. It made my voice hoarse.

She stood, her eyes narrowing. "What?"

"It's over with Krissy," I said. "What you said, about me never being able to see my son, I couldn't take it. I made the choice. I want to be with you."

I thought for sure she'd see right through the lies, that there was no way she could believe them for a single second. How could she? After all that had happened between us, how could she think that I wanted her?

"Kiss me."

It was a demand, not a request, and I could see on her face that she didn't even consider that I could be lying. When I'd said before that she was a narcissist, I hadn't understood just how right I was. She wasn't just self-absorbed. She was delusional, too.

I gestured towards the boy. "Not in front of the kid." I forced a smile, the kind of cocky, arrogant smile that used to be my usual. It was the look of a man who always got what he wanted, and what he usually wanted was sex. "In case things heat up."

Lust shone in her eyes as she turned to the boy. "Go into your room. Don't come out until I tell you to." She smiled at me. "You might want to put on some headphones or something. Things might get loud."

I was sickened at the realization that she thought I would fuck her here, rough and hard as I used to, with the boy in the next room. The boy she claimed was our son. The worst part was he didn't seem fazed by the order. I didn't even want to think about how many times she'd had the boy – Joey, I told myself, his name was Joey – leave the room so she could get off. One of the things that had appealed to me before had been her insatiable appetite. I knew she hadn't gone three years without scratching that itch.

"Now, DeVon, I think it's time we get reacquainted." She pulled off her tank top. "Fuck me."

It was odd, I thought, how she could be so demanding, but I knew what she would respond to best. I'd never wanted to be this man again, but I slipped him back on easily and heard the words come out of my mouth in the same harsh tone I'd once known so well.

"Are you telling me what to do? Get on your knees."

I walked over to the chair as she dropped to her knees. The look on her face said this was exactly what she'd wanted. I just hoped the cops would get here before things went too far. As much as I loved sex, I didn't want it with her.

There was one way to drag things out. One of the things that Sasha had always liked doing was hearing herself talk. I really didn't want her to answer the question I was about to ask, but better to hear it than have to act it out.

"What do you want me to do to you?" I settled in the chair like I was planning on being there for a while. I ran my hand over my stomach, then down further, letting my fingers brush the bulge in my jeans. My cock was completely soft, but Sasha didn't need to know that.

"I want you to whip me. My breasts, my ass, my clit." She shuffled forward a bit, her breasts jiggling with the movement. "Use a belt on me. I want you to fuck my mouth."

I heard the faint sound of sirens a moment before they cut off. Sasha didn't seem to have noticed. That was good. Now I just needed to keep her going a little bit longer.

"I've heard that all before." I made myself sound bored rather than disgusted. "In six years, haven't you learned anything new?"

She scowled at me and I wondered if I'd gone too far.

"I was pregnant and had a child during that time." Her tone was petulant, but I recognized it.

I raised an eyebrow. "And you're telling me that stopped you? I know you, Sasha. You could never go long without a nice, thick cock inside you. Without someone abusing those pretty tits of yours. Come on, be honest."

A sly smile curved her lips. "There are plenty of men with a taste for women in a, shall we say, certain way?"

I almost broke right there but, fortunately, that was the moment the door burst open and half a dozen cops streamed in, weapons drawn, shouting for everyone to put their hands up. Behind them, I saw Krissy next to an older cop who seemed to be barking out orders as to who was actually the bad guy in the room. I ignored all that. All I cared about was Krissy's eyes meeting mine and seeing there that we were okay. I nodded at her and she smiled at me.

It was over.

DeVon had insisted he go with Officer Purdue to get Emmett slash Joey. He said that since he was the only one of us who'd met the boy, it'd be better for him to be there. Everyone also agreed that it'd be best to wait to bring him out until after Sasha had been taken away. The biggest problem the cops were having with her was the fact that she wasn't wearing a shirt and wouldn't hold still long enough for anyone to get anything on her, and no one wanted to deal with the legal ramifications of marching her out of the hotel half-naked. Her hands were already cuffed behind her, which wasn't helping, but they hadn't had a choice. She'd been going after everyone with her nails. Finally, DeVon went into one of the bedrooms, found a long-sleeved shirt and forced it over her head. He wrapped the arms around her waist and then tied them in place, further restraining her.

I was actually kind of surprised that she wasn't more violent with him or hadn't spit on him. Instead, she just talked. And talked. And talked. Curses. Threats. What she was going to do to all of us, especially me. The moment I'd walked in, she'd started in on me. She shared all of the things she and DeVon had done together, all of the explicit details of the week they'd been together. I was pretty sure the cops didn't believe her considering she looked like a raving lunatic, but I knew the things DeVon liked and I was equally as certain that most of what she said was the truth. I didn't care.

Finally, the cops dragged her out of the room and Officer Purdue went with DeVon to get the boy. This time, when I saw him, I didn't look for similarities to DeVon but rather to the picture of Joey Turner. It had been a little over three years since that picture had been taken, but I could see it. The shape of his eyes, their color. His hair was longer than it had been, but still had a cowlick in the same place. His face still had some of its baby roundness and I wondered whether if Sasha'd had him a bit longer, he'd have lost enough of that for the resemblance to wane.

DeVon and I rode back to the police station with Joey. Fingerprints and a DNA swab would be done for one hundred percent certainty, but I didn't think anyone doubted that this was Joey Turner. Officer Purdue made the call from the car. He kept it brief and vague enough that Joey wouldn't be able to tell what it was about.

The boy was quiet for the entire ride, sitting between DeVon and me with a blank expression on his face. It didn't really surprise me, though. Before we'd left the hotel, the police had found bottles of tranquilizers. It didn't take a detective to guess that Joey's detached behavior was most likely drug-induced. DeVon had said Joey had been sleeping when he'd first gone to the room and I'd seen enough pill-popping socialites to know how groggy they looked after waking up from a drugged sleep. Hell, half of my morning memories of my mother had her looking like that.

By the time we got to the station, Joey was alert enough to know that something was going on. When he asked about Sasha, we told him only that she was going to go away for a long time. The relieved look on his face said that there had been more fear in their relationship than attachment.

"What's going to happen to me?" he asked as the three of us walked into the police station.

Out of the corner of my eye, I caught a handful of reporters heading our way. Apparently, the word had gotten out. I hurried DeVon and Joey along until we were in the safety of the building.

"Someone here is going to tell you that," DeVon said, glancing at me.

I knew what he was thinking. It would've been hard enough to have the "I'm your dad" conversation. This one was way out of our depth.

"Hello." A kind-looking, middle-aged woman approached. The folder tucked under her arm told me she was the social worker on call. The fact that she barely greeted DeVon and me and went straight to Joey made me like her. "My name's Madeleine and I'm going to tell you what's going on. Will that be all right?"

Joey glanced up at DeVon and then at me. "Can they come with me?"

Madeleine gave a quick look toward one of the officers who nodded. "If that's what you want."

I wasn't sure I wanted to be there when everything came out, but if Joey was brave enough to hear it, so was I. The four of us went into a small side room and waited a few moments while Officer Purdue took Joey's fingerprints. DeVon and I sat on the couch while Madeleine began to talk to Joey, asking him about things that he remembered about his younger years. She started recently and went further and further back until he finally said that he couldn't remember anything else.

DeVon reached for my hand, threading his fingers between

mine. I could feel the tension radiating off of him. It didn't sound like Sasha had abused Joey, but she had definitely been neglectful. His memories were almost all sad and lonely ones, each one tearing at my heart. I suddenly wanted to go down to whatever holding cell they had Sasha in and beat the shit out of her. Not for the first time, I thought that it was a good idea I hadn't gone into criminal law.

Madeleine's eyes flicked up to the door when Officer Purdue cracked it open. He simply nodded once, confirming what we'd already known. Madeleine looked at DeVon and me as she knelt in front of Joey and took his hands. I knew she was about to tell him the truth. Nothing in what he'd said indicated that he remembered that Sasha wasn't his real mother. This was going to destroy everything he'd ever known.

DeVon's hand tightened almost painfully around mine.

"What I'm going to tell you may sound scary or not true, but I want you to trust me, okay?" Her voice was gentle. She waited until he nodded. "The woman you were with, three years ago, she took a little boy named Joey Turner from his parents."

Joey's eyes widened and I thought I caught a glimpse of recognition at the name.

"Joey's parents have been very sad and have been looking for him all this time." She paused a moment before continuing, "I know that woman said she was your mother and that your name was Emmett, but that's not the truth. Your real name is Joey Turner and your real parents are flying here from Minnesota. They are so happy you're okay."

Silence fell as we all waited for Joey's reaction.

"She wasn't my mom?" His voice was quiet.

"No," Madeleine kept it simple.

"I never have to live with her again?"

A lump formed in my throat as I heard the hope in his voice.

"No. You're never going to live with her again."

"And I have parents. A real mom and dad?"

"Yes."

A wide smile broke out across his face and he threw his arms around Madeleine. "Thank you!"

We stayed for another half-hour, wanting to be sure Joey was comfortable before we left. His parents had left St. Paul as soon as they'd been able to get on a flight, but it'd be at least four hours before they arrived. Neither DeVon nor I had the energy to stay that long. My heart twisted as Joey threw his arms around DeVon to tell him good-bye. I couldn't imagine how DeVon must have been feeling at that moment. He'd been through so much. Thinking he had a son. Being told he'd have to choose between me and the boy. Then learning that the child he'd been thinking of as his, wasn't.

As the two of us left, I slid my arm around his waist and leaned my head on his shoulder. "I'm so sorry, babe."

"For what?" he sounded tired, but curious.

"I just feel bad about what happened. Everything you had to go through these past two weeks, only to find out you have to give him up anyway."

Our usual driver gave us both concerned looks as he opened the back door of the town car. I managed a small smile before sliding in. I was glad DeVon had called for a car. I wanted some privacy right now.

"It was bittersweet, you know." DeVon put his arm around my shoulders and pulled me against him. "Finding out that Emmett – I mean, Joey – wasn't my son."

"Really?" I kept my voice carefully neutral.

"I'm really glad I didn't have a kid with Sasha, and I'm even more grateful that she's not anyone's mother."

That was a sentiment I could definitely agree with. Some people should never reproduce.

"But I was just starting to get used to the idea of being someone's dad."

I pushed myself up straight so I could look at him. This was a conversation I needed to have face-to-face.

"Had you ever thought of it before?" I knew he'd been engaged when he was younger, but he and I had never talked about what he thought about having kids. I wished we had.

"Not really," he said. "Family always seemed like it'd be more of Franco's thing than mine. Look how long it took me to figure out that I could be happy with just one person." He smiled at me. "As long as it's you."

I gave him a weak smile in return. "Good thing you added that last part."

"Besides, Joey is a great kid. Anyone would be proud to have him as a son, no matter if they wanted kids or not. He's smart and sweet. Especially when you consider how hard it must've been, growing up thinking Sasha was his mother, it's a miracle he's not completely screwed up."

I nodded absently. I agreed that Joey had to be a special kid indeed to have done so well with such a nutcase, but he wasn't at the forefront of my mind at the moment. I put my hand on my stomach. Was that it? Had he only decided that he wanted to be Joey's dad because of what a great kid Joey was? Even now, was DeVon thinking about how nice it was going to be to go back to the way things had been? Just the two of us with work and our houses and amazing sex.

"Babe?" He brushed the back of his fingers across my cheek. "What's wrong?"

This wasn't where or how I'd wanted to have this conversation, but the moment had presented itself and I had to know the truth. I couldn't settle back down into a routine with him if he didn't want things to change.

"Did you only want Joey because he's such a great kid and

he was already here? Was it only because, short of walking away, you didn't really have a choice in the matter?"

He cupped the side of my face. "No. Meeting him just made me consider the idea, forced me to decide what I want."

"And what's that?" The question came out in a near-whisper. I almost didn't want to hear the answer.

"I don't want kids," he began and my heart nearly stopped. "Unless they're with you."

I took a shaky breath, not wanting to dare to hope.

"It's not about having a son or daughter," he continued. "It's about being a family, and you're the only person I'd ever want to have a family with."

Tears spilled over and I cursed my hormones. "That's good," I said as relief rushed through me. DeVon's bewildered expression made me laugh.

"It's good because I'm pregnant."

I was pretty sure our driver thought DeVon and I were crazy as
we got out of the town car laughing and kissing each other, especially considering how somber we'd been getting in. He was
professional, though, and merely gave us a nod and got back into
the car.

I was glad we'd gone back to the house because this was
where I wanted to celebrate. I liked the penthouse and I knew it
was a good idea to have it, but this house was where I wanted to
raise our child.

I'd barely gone three steps towards the door and DeVon was
scooping me up in his arms, laughing when I gave a surprised
sound that I vehemently denied was a squeal. I wrapped my
arms around his neck as he carried me into the house and
directly to the master bathroom.

He undressed me quickly and efficiently, not taking the
time to linger before stripping off his own clothes. The water
was hot as we stepped under it and it felt amazing against my
tense muscles. One of the best things about central air was the
ability to still take a hot shower in July.

As he reached for my shampoo, he asked, "I am curious,

though. How did it happen?"

I picked up his shampoo as I teased, "Well, when two people love each other very much..."

He laughed. "You know what I mean. And don't get me wrong, I'm thrilled. Just curious."

"Let's just say there's a birth control company that didn't recall their product fast enough and are going to have a whole lot of lawsuits on their hands soon."

"Maybe we should send them a thank you card," he joked.

We lathered each other's hair, the mood light as we rinsed and he then worked conditioner through my thick mess.

"How far along...I mean, when...?"

"I'm guessing sometime in April," I answered the question he hadn't actually managed to get out. "I haven't been to the doctor yet."

"You have to schedule the appointment right away," he said. His previous playfulness had disappeared. "We need to make sure everything's okay."

I squirted soap into a washcloth. "No one's open today. I'll call on Monday." I began to make small circles across the defined muscles of his chest.

"Do we want to know if it's a boy or a girl?" He frowned. "Should we wait until then to start talking about names? Which room's going to be the nursery? Do you want to go with the traditional pink or blue or should we do something more neutral in case we want more kids? Do you want more kids?"

"DeVon," I interrupted him. A smile was playing around my lips, but I didn't want him to think I was laughing at him. "We don't need to make all of those decisions right now. We've got time to talk about them."

"Nine months goes by really fast," he said. He looked down at me. "What if something goes wrong?"

"Shh." I walked around him and began to wash his back. "We're not going to worry about that."

He watched me finish cleaning him, his eyes dark and full of so much love that it was almost painful to bear. When I was done, he poured my lilac-scented soap onto another washcloth and began to mimic what I'd done. His movements were slow and gentle. Unlike other times when we'd showered together, there was no teasing, no sexual advances.

Then he went to his knees to wash my legs and feet. I put my hands on his shoulders to balance, expecting him to stand as he finished, but he didn't. He looked up at me, his thick lashes dotted with water. His hands slid around me to the small of my back as he looked back down. I caught my breath as he pressed his lips against my stomach and then turned his head, resting his cheek against me. I moved my arms so they were behind his neck, holding him against me.

We stood there for what seemed like a long time and then he stood. Neither one of us spoke as we rinsed the last of the soap off and then climbed out of the shower. He toweled me off first and it was all I could do not to lean forward and lick the drops of water off of his chest and abs. I tucked my towel tightly around me and moved to return the favor.

"No," he said quietly as he took his towel.

Not that I didn't enjoy watching him dry himself off, I was curious. "Why not?"

He smiled at me. "Because if you do that, I'm going to want to do more than sleep when we get in bed."

I grinned. "That sounds good to me."

A pained expression crossed his face. "I...I don't want to hurt you. Or the baby."

"DeVon, we're not going to stop having sex for the next nine months. It's okay."

"Krissy–"

"We'll ask the doctor some specifics, but I can promise you that we can still make love." I took a step backwards towards the door and reached for the edge of the towel. "Unless, of course, you're not interested anymore." I let the towel fall.

DeVon made a sound in the back of his throat. I smiled and cupped my breasts. My nipples hardened with just a light touch. I shivered. I'd suspected before that they were more sensitive. Now I knew for sure. That was going to make things fun. When I ran my hand down my stomach, DeVon's eyes followed.

"In which case," I continued my taunt. "I'll just have to take care of this myself."

With a growl, DeVon stalked towards me, his cock already hardening. I laughed and ran for the bed, barely making it before he grabbed my hips and turned me to face him. He cupped the back of my head and took my mouth with a fierce possessiveness that took my breath away. His tongue tangled with mine as he lowered me onto our bed.

Our bed. Our house. Our baby.

I pulled him down on me. I didn't want foreplay and sweet torture before he slid inside me. I just wanted him. I wrapped my legs around his waist and reached down between us. He groaned into my mouth as I wrapped my fingers around him.

"Wait," he gasped. "Let me go down on you first."

"No." I shook my head even as I squeezed the firm flesh in my hand. "I'm wet enough."

His eyes locked with mine and I saw that his need was just as great. After everything that had happened, what we were doing wasn't about the pleasure. It was about us joining together, becoming one.

I released his cock and he entered me. My eyelids fluttered, my nails digging into his shoulders at the nearly overwhelming sensation of initial penetration. I let him take me slow, reveling in each exquisite inch that stretched me. My entire body was thrumming, like every cell was tuning in to the same frequency, one that responded to his touch and nothing else.

He didn't stop when he reached the end of me, but began to withdraw almost immediately. The steady drag made me moan, and then his lips were surrounding a nipple and the moan became a cry. My back arched as he began to suck, his body curling over mine as his tongue and teeth worked the sensitive flesh even as he maintained his pace.

Fireworks burst behind my eyes and I called out his name, an orgasm exploding through me. He swore as my pussy tightened around him, my muscles spasming as I came. He waited until I'd begun to come down before he started to move again, this time with more force, though not even close to his usual pounding. He raised his head until our eyes met.

We didn't speak. We didn't have to. We could see everything the other one was feeling and it was the exact image of what we felt. We truly were soulmates. Everything about us fit perfectly together. Our bodies, hearts and minds. Everything we'd never thought we'd want or have, but now did.

We came together, not with a bang or a whimper, but with a rush of love and desire so intense that it took our breath away. We clung to each other, our bodies as closely entwined as a pair could be, riding the waves of pleasure until we both had tears in our eyes. Even then, we didn't pull apart. Only when the chill of the air conditioning began to reach us did we untangle long enough to slide underneath the blankets.

DeVon lay on his side next to me, his head propped up on one hand. His other hand was lazily caressing my curves beneath the sheet, sliding over each of my breasts before settling on my stomach.

"You know it's too early to feel anything," I said as I traced his jaw with my finger.

"I know." He nipped at my finger, smiling as I dropped my hand to his chest. "But he's in there. Or she." He snuggled down next to me and pulled me into his arms, still managing to get a hand on my stomach. "It doesn't matter to me which. Maybe one of each."

I turned my head to glare at him. "Twins? Seriously?"

He grinned. "Go big or go home, right?"

My eyes narrowed even more. "You do realize that using the word 'big' in a sentence with a pregnant woman is a dangerous thing, right?"

He winked at me. "Does this mean you're going to have to punish me?"

I loved DeVon dominating me, but I couldn't deny the bolt of arousal that went through me at the idea of him in the submissive role for once. I filed that away for future reference.

"One, two, boy, girl, it doesn't matter." He brushed my hair back and kissed my forehead. "And I don't care how big you get or how weird your cravings are. You're perfect. They'll be perfect. No matter what."

I rested my head on his chest, listening to my favorite sound in the world.

"Because you're mine." His arms tightened around me. "My family. The only thing I'll ever need."

I wanted to tell him that I felt the same way, but I was already half-asleep. It could wait, though. I'd tell him tomorrow. And the day after that. Neither one of us was going anywhere. We were a family. Always.

**The Club Privé series continues in *Unlawful Attraction (Club Privé Book 7)*. Turn the page for a free preview.**

# UNLAWFUL ATTRACTION
## PREVIEW

# ONE

## DENA

The woman in the mirror looked back at me with pale gray eyes that matched the suit. It was a good suit, one I wore when I needed to look at least close to my twenty-six years, or when I wanted to look my best. Since today was my last day at Webster & Steinberg, it was my only choice.

I couldn't believe it was finally here. I'd gone through the follow-ups with my biggest clients and handled the ones who needed to be gently handed off to the woman who'd fill my shoes. They'd all been sorry to see me go, but not as sorry as my boss. I'd be the fourth lawyer she lost in a little over a year. The other three had been friends of mine, and their absence here made leaving a bit easier.

I thoroughly expected to get through the day without anyone really noticing and I'd managed it up until a few minutes ago when my co-workers had sprung a surprise going-away party for me. Surprise because I wasn't really that close with any of them. Without Leslie, Carrie and Krissy here, I'd mostly kept to myself. I wasn't shy or a snob, but I liked to focus on my work, and they'd been the only ones who'd ever really managed to keep me from being a total workaholic.

The bathroom door swung open and I leaned forward to finish checking my make-up. I hadn't cried because I didn't do that, but I had gotten a bit teary and I wanted to make sure nothing had run.

Emma smiled at me as she came in. "Don't think for one moment we're going to let you hide in here."

I gave her a small smile. "I thought for once you guys wouldn't make a big deal of things."

"You're such a sweet kid, believing in fairy tales." She winked at me before disappearing into one of the stalls.

I laughed and affably called her a bitch before stepping back from the counter. With my white blonde hair chopped into a short pixie-cut and my petite frame, I looked years younger than I was, which meant I spent plenty of time being referred to as a 'kid.' Instead of letting it bother me, I usually took advantage of people underestimating me.

"By the way, Dena, one of the partners came down to tell you good-bye. Better get out there," she added.

Sighing, I pushed away from the sink. "Why would they want to do that?" I'd already said good-bye to my boss, Mimi. She wasn't a named partner, but rumor had it she would be by the end of the year.

Emma answered my question, "Probably because you know exactly when to go for the balls and exactly how hard to squeeze. You'll be missed. For your ability to squeeze balls if nothing else."

I rolled my eyes as I turned toward the door.

Another hour and I'd be done. I both dreaded and anticipated the moment. I'd miss the stability, the familiarity of Webster & Steinberg, but at the same time, I'd been preparing for the step I was about to take for what felt like my entire life.

As soon as I stepped out of the bathroom, scents of food assailed me from the break room. My belly started to rumble almost immediately. They'd kept me running all day, so when I hadn't been finishing up with my clients, I'd been handling busy work or running errands, even making calls that generally the interns would've handled. I hadn't thought anything of it since I'd known I couldn't take on anything new.

Now I saw they'd kept me busy so I wouldn't figure out what they were up to. It also meant I hadn't had a chance to eat lunch. Most people thought that since I was barely five feet and maybe a hundred pounds that I didn't eat much. That wasn't the case, and I was seriously hungry.

As I stepped into the break room, the decorations hit me all over again. The entire room was done up in streamers, and on the far wall there was a sign with bars that read *Put 'em away, Dena!* Behind the bars, it showed the scruffy, tired face of a man glaring sullenly at the camera.

Two weeks ago, I'd accepted a position as an assistant district attorney. I wouldn't be arguing the big cases or anything. Not for a while yet, but at least I had the ever important foot in the door. Once I'd proven myself, I'd get to start on the big stuff.

"Are you excited?"

At the question, I looked over at Lori Martin, the attorney the firm had hired to take my clients. Since Leslie had left a couple months back, I carried too heavy a load to just shunt my cases off onto others in the firm. The divorce business was booming.

Smiling at Lori, I nodded. "I am."

For as long as I could remember, this was all I ever wanted to do. Some little girls grew up dreaming about being a nurse, a doctor, a teacher. Not me.

A friend of mine from high school had majored in archaeology. That had been her dream ever since she'd been a kid. Working in the garden with her mom one year, she'd found a bone and in her child's mind, it had been a bone from some rare, undiscovered dinosaur. In reality, it'd been a dog's hind leg, but that hadn't mattered in the long run. It sparked her interest and she'd gone for it.

I'd always wanted to be a lawyer. A prosecutor, to be specific. Working at Webster & Steinberg had only been a stepping stone.

Unfortunately, I didn't have some fun little story about why I'd decided I wanted to put bad guys away. My desire had come from tragedy.

Late one night, more than twenty years ago, sirens had woken me. I'd crawled into bed with my parents and gone back to sleep. As a child, that wailing sound had been common enough in my neighborhood.

The next morning, both of my parents had been unusually quiet. My father had gone to work like usual, but Mom stayed home with me. When I asked her why my sitter hadn't come yet, she told me my sitter had gone away. I persisted, but all she'd say was that Miss Jenny was gone and I'd understand when I was older.

The problem was, I'd always been a precocious child, too nosy for my own good, and I discovered the truth myself a couple of days later when I'd seen a newspaper with a picture of Jenny.

Mom had come in when I'd been sounding out the headline.

She'd tried to take the paper away, but I'd already figured out enough of the words to ask the question.

*What's dead, Mama?*

My mother had softened the blow as much as she could, but how could anything about murder be soft to a four year-old? I'd understood sick and old, but I'd known Miss Jenny hadn't been either one of those.

Mom told me that the man who'd killed Miss Jenny had been a different kind of sick and that he hadn't meant it. My childish mind had accepted that, but I'd come back to her explanation years later when the older sister of a boy in my class had been murdered. At twelve, I'd been old enough to read the stories in the newspapers and online. And I'd been old enough to research when I recognized the name of the man's previous victim.

Jennifer Kyle.

That's when I'd found out that Jenny's killer had been an ex who'd beaten her before. That he'd been arrested with her blood still on him, but a defense attorney had found a loophole that had let the murderer go free. Free to kill my classmate's sister.

That was when I'd decided what I wanted to do with my life. I wanted to be the one who made the bad guys go to jail.

Soon, I'd be doing it. Very soon.

Looking over at Lori, I nodded again. "Yes. I'm very excited."

MY EXCITEMENT MUST'VE BEEN SHOWING on my face when I walked into Club Privé that night. My friends were already waiting for me at our regular table, Carrie's and Krissy's men at their sides. Carrie and her extremely rich and hot fiancé, Gavin Manning, ran the club together and they were almost sickeningly in love. Not that Krissy and her equally gorgeous and wealthy man, DeVon, were any better. They both lived on the West Coast, but DeVon was rich enough that he and Krissy came to visit as often as possible.

I hugged Leslie first as she stood to push out my chair. Krissy was next, and then I was in Carrie's arms for a quick, but heartfelt embrace.

I didn't have a chance for anything more than that, though.

Carrie's eyes narrowed as she released me. "You're up to

something. It's written all over your face, Dena. Tell us. What is it? Tell us."

Krissy leaned forward a little bit, her expression speculative.

Shit. I'd forgotten how intuitive the two of them could be. Even Leslie was looking at me with suspicion, and she usually let me alone.

"You're right, Carrie," Krissy agreed, nodding sagely. "You're up to something, Dena. I know that smirk. What's going on?"

I reached for the glass of water in front of me and took a sip, trying to buy time. I didn't want to just blurt it out. These three women were my best friends, the closest things I'd ever had to sisters. They would understand why this was so important to me.

In those brief seconds, Krissy took over, falling easily into her usual role within the group. Her dark eyes glinted as she propped her elbow on the table. Chin in hand, she asked, "Did you meet a guy? Say you met a guy. Tall and blond, or dark and mysterious?"

"Both?" Leslie wiggled her eyebrows suggestively. At least with her there, I wasn't the only single one.

With a snort, I glanced over as a woman stopped by to check on our drinks. I put my order in before answering, "No. I didn't meet a guy." Mentally, I added, *I wish.*

I'd hooked up with a couple men off and on over the past year, but none of them had been worth more than one night. A part of me wanted what Krissy and Carrie had, but it wasn't as easy for me as it was for them.

I wasn't exactly blaming myself for my single state, but I had certain...quirks that made it hard for anything long-term. Club Privé, ideally, should've made it easier, but in reality, it hadn't.

There were plenty of good-looking guys – and hell, I wasn't so

UNLAWFUL ATTRACTION PREVIEW    155

shallow that the man had to be a ten. Other things mattered besides washboard abs and a face that looked like he'd been carved by the very hands of Michelangelo. I *did* want somebody I was physically attracted to, but somebody who made me laugh and somebody who *got* me did a hell of a lot more than a pretty face.

And that was where everything got fucked up.

Club Privé was a sex club, and one that catered to the bdsm lifestyle. Except most of the guys who came here already had it in their head what they wanted from a sub, and I didn't fit that role. Oh, I might've looked the part, but there weren't a lot of men who had what it took to dominate a switch. And that's what I was.

Some of the time, I loved being in control in the bedroom, but there a lot of times I needed something else. It freed something inside me, gave me a place where I could just let go and know that I'd be taken care of. But it'd been way too long since I'd had that.

The men who saw that I could also dominate took it as a challenge, something to work out of me, especially the men who got off on humiliation as a way to top their partner. I didn't judge the ones who were into that, but it wasn't my kink. Sub or Dom, I enjoyed the control part of things. A little rough play wasn't bad, but the whole punishment / humiliation part of things wasn't what I wanted.

So, more often than not, I ended up on top. And while that did speak to my control-freak side, it didn't do that much for the part of me who wanted to be taken care of.

Feeling the watchful eyes of my friends, I glanced up and smiled a little ruefully. "No. No guy. I wish that was my surprise." I gave a lusty sigh. "Man, do I ever wish."

"But there is a surprise?" Leslie asked.

"Well..." I drew the word out, not bothering to fight my grin.

"Yes. Usually, you two are the ones with all the good news and stuff, but it's my turn."

Across the glossy surface of the big, round table, Krissy and DeVon shared a secretive little smile. Or at least, Krissy had a secretive smile on her face when she looked over at him. He smiled back at her, but he just looked laid back and relaxed as he traced his fingers over the skin of her arm.

Reaching for my wineglass, I asked, "All right, you two. What's going on?"

"No, no, no. You have news. I want to hear your news." Krissy shook her head emphatically, her eyes sparkling.

I glanced at DeVon. Maybe he wasn't grinning the way she was, but his dark brown eyes had a glint to them, and there was definitely something different in the looks he was giving her. I was used to him looking at her like he couldn't wait to find somewhere private he could do some seriously naughty things to her, but these looks were different. Gentle, awed.

I glanced over at Carrie and she shrugged. "Beats me. She's been all giggly ever since she got here, and she won't say anything. Now spill your news before I have to beat it out of you."

Gavin nuzzled Carrie's neck. "Can we watch?" He winked at me, a playful gesture that had absolutely no heat to it.

Carrie elbowed him sharply and he kissed her cheek. I would've suggested they get a room, but they probably would've done exactly that and disappeared for the rest of the night.

I rolled my eyes. "Okay, I'll spill." I may have sounded like they were twisting my arm, but I knew my friends didn't believe it for a minute. I allowed myself another dramatic pause. "As of today, I'm unemployed."

All five of them exchanged glances that ranged from worried to confused.

Unsurprisingly, it was Krissy who spoke first. "Okay. I don't get it. You look happy. Having a job is a good thing, right?"

"It is." I smiled and continued, "Technically, I guess you could say I'm only temporarily unemployed. First thing Monday, I'm starting my new job as an assistant district attorney."

They stared at me for a moment as they processed the news, and then the women erupted. Krissy practically climbed over DeVon to get out of the booth while Carrie wrapped me up in a tight hug. Leslie was next, her squeal loud enough to make the nearest table stare at us. I didn't care though. As Krissy joined in the group hug, I closed my eyes and sighed.

I might not have had a fantastic guy, but I was getting ready to start my dream job and I had great friends. Life was good.

---

"I THINK her bladder has shrunk down to the size of a peanut," Carrie said as she scrolled through her iPad, showing me pictures of some of the places she and Gavin were planning on going for their honeymoon.

Krissy had been looking at pictures with the rest of us, but now she was in the bathroom for the third time.

I studied the serene, blue-green waters on the screen before glancing up at Carrie. "I'm dying of envy, you know."

"Take a vacation and go. You don't need a guy to go on vacation," Carrie said.

"But they do make some things more fun," Leslie put in with a wicked grin. "You could pick one up over there in a heartbeat. Get your brains fucked out. You probably need it." She nudged me with her elbow, green eyes shining.

Rolling my eyes, I shook my head. "It'll be a little bit before I get a decent vacation. Starting a new job, remember?"

"Doesn't mean you can't pick up a hottie to have some fun with right here," Leslie said. She tossed her red curls over her shoulder and surveyed the prospects again.

Across from us, DeVon caught my attention by getting to his feet. Even if that hadn't been a clue, I would've known by the way his face softened that Krissy was coming back from the bathroom.

As she took her seat next to him, I glanced at her. "That's like your third trip to powder your nose, honey."

"A girl must always look her best," she said primly. She gestured to the tablet. "Carrie still teasing us with her honey-moon plans?"

"It's not teasing," Carrie huffed. "It's *sharing*."

"Teasing, sharing. It's all the same thing," Krissy made a dismissive gesture with her hand.

"If you want to go on a fantastic trip with your man, nobody's stopping you." Carrie waved loftily in DeVon's direction.

"No, travel is something we won't be doing for a while." Krissy looked up at the man sitting next to her and stroked her hand across his arm. He gave her a slight nod. "As a matter of fact, in a few months we won't even be able to travel out here much."

DeVon slid his arm around her shoulders and leaned over to kiss the top of her head.

I frowned as I looked at Leslie and Carrie who looked as lost as I was. "Is everything okay?" I asked.

It seemed like a stupid question. Krissy looked fine. She was smiling, her face glowing. And it wasn't like she was drunk or anything. I glanced at her glass. All Krissy had sipped on all night was water...

"Son of a bitch. You're pregnant." The words popped out without me realizing that I was planning on saying them.

"Seriously?" Leslie asked with a raised eyebrow.

"Take a look." I pointed at Krissy's glass. "No alcohol. Three bathroom trips in just a couple hours. Travel restrictions. And the two of them have been practically purring over something all night."

Carrie, Gavin and Leslie looked at Krissy and DeVon. The matching smiles on their faces confirmed everything I was saying. Leslie squealed again as we all moved to hug our friends.

Babies and marriages and new jobs. It seemed like my little group of friends and I were all moving toward new chapters in our lives, and I was more than ready to see what the future held.

# TWO
## DENA

Krissy and DeVon had left nearly half an hour ago. They were leaving in the morning so they could stop over in Chicago to tell Krissy's family the good news. Leslie had been on the prowl for a while, but seemed to be setting her sights on one dark-haired man who seemed to be thoroughly enjoying her attention. Carrie and Gavin were dancing somewhere, although he did occasionally have to stop to deal with business. She didn't seem to mind though. She seemed more at home here than she ever had at Webster & Steinberg.

Swaying on the dance floor, I contemplated my own prospects for the night. I hadn't spent time and money on the sexy little black number I was currently wearing just to hang out and watch my friends. With my petite build, I had to be careful I didn't pick things that made me look twelve, and I'd chosen this dress specifically because it didn't. Matched with a pair of four inch heels, I knew I looked good. Now I just had to find someone worth the effort that had gone into looking like this.

I'd already declined several offers when a sleek, chiseled guy approached me, his hands coming out to grasp my hips sure and confident. The way he moved would've given me high hopes if I hadn't already done this song and dance a hundred times before. At least it felt that way.

Lazily, I spun around on the floor, putting my back to his chest, enjoying the feel of his body moving against mine. It was a trick of mine, a way to gauge if I wanted to do anything more than share a dance with him. If he got all grabby then and there, then it would end here. There was a fine line between sensual and out-and-out groping.

He dipped his head and skimmed his lips along my bare shoulder.

I felt disconnected.

That didn't bode well.

His palm stroked up my side and I caught his wrist. Too bad.

"A little shy?" he murmured in my ear, just loud enough to be heard over the music.

"I prefer to think of myself as selective."

He chuckled, and I felt a warm puff of air against my ear. It didn't feel erotic. The gut instinct I relied on as both an attorney and a New Yorker told me this wasn't the right guy.

Still, I kept my movements easy as I swiveled around to look at him. I needed to see how he'd take me not melting in his arms.

He gave me a slow, sage nod as if his approval was somehow necessary. "I like that. Picky. You just need the right man to take you. Make you obedient. Break you until you're the perfect little submissive slave."

Was he serious? Any lust I'd been feeling vanished. Lip curling, I came to a stop in the middle of the dance floor.

"Break me?" I said. At that exact moment, the music fell into one of those odd lulls – the DJ switching to a different song, or an electrical issue – and those two words hung in the air.

I didn't normally care to be the center of attention unless I was addressing the court, but at that moment, I was too pissed off to care. As he took a step toward me, still smiling that smug smile, I let my disdain show through. The music started again, but the attention was still on me.

"*Break* me?" I said again. I hated men like this, the ones who gave the entire lifestyle a bad name. "Is that what you think this is about? Either you're new, or you never had a decent teacher, so let me give you some advice. Being a Dom has nothing to do with *breaking* anybody. Submission is all about willingly giving up control to someone you trust. Not someone who *broke* you."

His face bled to an ugly shade of red and he took another step toward me.

Suddenly, a large body stepped between me and the idiot. A glance up told me that it was one of the regulars, a Dom who was easily six and a half feet tall and built like a brick wall.

"I think you need to leave the lady alone," he said, towering over the much smaller man.

The wannabe Dom gave me a scathing look around the man between us before storming off. For a few seconds, the tension held, but then it was gone and everyone went back to what they'd been doing.

I thanked the man who helped me and smiled as I watched him walk away. A tall, muscular man was waiting and the two shared a sweet embrace that made something in my chest ache. It seemed like everyone but me could find what they needed.

---

TWENTY MINUTES and a glass and a half of wine later, Gavin found me brooding at the bar. "I showed that asshole to the door."

"Ugh," I groaned. "You didn't need to kick him out for me." Picking up my glass of wine, I swirled it around before meeting his gaze.

"It wasn't just for you. It was for everyone here. And for me."

Gavin leaned back against the bar, resting on his elbows. Not for the first time, I thought of how lucky Carrie was to have found him.

He continued, "Apparently, he was here on a guest VIP pass, trying the package out. After you shut him down, he came stomping up to me and got in my face, wanting to know why the subs weren't better trained." Amusement danced in his deep blue eyes. "Dena, why aren't you better trained?"

I chuckled, and then asked, "Was Carrie around when he asked that?"

"Yeah, she was." He grinned at me.

I burst out laughing, my melancholy mood gone. He leaned over and kissed my cheek. "I thought that would make you smile."

Someone called his name and he headed off, but I wasn't left alone long. When somebody settled down next to me, I glanced over, a dismissal already forming on my lips. I'd already decided I wasn't up to messing around tonight.

But then I met a pair of soft blue eyes and something stayed my tongue.

"Hello."

The man's gaze fell away for a brief moment, and then he looked at me and smiled.

"I enjoyed your show on the dance floor."

"That wasn't meant to be a show." I gave him a wry smile before taking another sip of wine.

"I figured as much." He quickly brushed his fingers across the back of my hand before pulling away, his eyes dropping for another moment. "Are you looking for company tonight?"

I took my time deliberating the question. This guy wasn't

exactly what I'd been planning on, but no one had been lately. Besides, he looked like he might be fun.

---

PRIVATE ROOMS at Club Privé were nothing short of amazing to begin with. As a VIP member and one of Carrie's best friends, I had access to the best of the best.

In this case, it involved a room where I could stretch myself out on a king-size bed, while the sub who'd approached me knelt between my thighs and went to work on me like there was nothing else he would rather do than lick me straight into orgasm.

And he was damn *good* at it too.

After he'd brought me to a second climax, he paused, his cheek on my thigh as his breath came in rough, ragged gasps. I propped myself up on my elbows and looked down my body to meet Jack's blue eyes.

"Would you like another?" He licked his lips, clearly having enjoyed himself as much as I had.

I did, actually, because the first two had been wonderful, but what I really wanted was his cock. Absently, I tried to remember the last time I'd been the one on my knees, a man's hands fisted tightly in my hair while he thrust his cock past my lips, deep into my mouth until I couldn't take him deeper – and then he had me take just a little more.

I could've gone down on Jack, felt the weight of him on my tongue, but it wouldn't have been the same. There was a term, 'topping from the bottom' that could've worked, where I was technically still dominating the sub, but performing various things that one would normally consider to be the function of a sub.

It wasn't the actions I wanted though. I wanted the loss of control. But since I couldn't have that, I'd have him.

Sitting up, I fisted a hand in Jack's dark hair. He made a small sound in the back of his throat.

"I think what I want right now is for you to get on the bench over there."

"What do you plan to do to me?" Jack asked, voice ragged.

The excitement in his voice was palpable, and something monstrously close to envy burned inside me. Pushing my initial plan aside, I didn't answer him. "I changed my mind. Kneel down in front of the bench. Facing it."

His long, lean body flushed as he moved to do as I said. His cock was hard and he hadn't even touched it. I knew he was waiting for me to tell him it was okay, but we weren't there yet. Since I'd brought him up here, I'd agreed, even if it had been silently, to take care of his needs. That's what a good Dom did, made sure their sub was taken care of.

As he knelt down in front of the bench, I moved to the wall with its display of various tools and toys. Upon using one, it would be added to my account and I could either take it home, or they'd keep it for me for the next time. I took my time and found a crop that was both functional and elegant.

What could I say? I was a girl who liked having pretty toys.

Testing it against my hand, I glanced over to find him staring at me in the mirror.

The naked heat and raw desire in his eyes fired that part of me that did enjoy the domination side of things, and I turned, walking lazily over to him. Pressing the end of the crop to his neck, I nudged him forward.

"Bend over."

After he complied, I took a moment to admire the designs tattooed across his skin. I traced them with the tip of the crop and watched goosebumps break out across his skin. When he was practically shivering in anticipation, I lifted the crop then brought it down across his muscled ass. He tensed, a harsh noise escaping him.

I knew that sound. It wasn't one of pain, but rather the sound that someone made when pain had been relieved. My gut clenched and I pushed aside my own desire for that same relief.

I brought the crop down again, this time on his right flank.

Another tight sound escaped him followed by a shudder.

I settled into a pattern that alternated from side to side, working up and down from his buttocks to a few inches above his knees, staying away from the joints where it could cause damage.

He was moaning and writhing, demanding sounds falling harshly from his lips. He was panting, begging, swearing...but never once did he say the safe word we'd agreed on.

Finally, I brought the crop to my side and moved forward, straddling the bench. "Sit up," I ordered.

He did, swaying a bit, his eyes glazed with the headspace that came with someone thoroughly into what we were doing. I waited until he was steady, watching to make sure I didn't need to help him maintain his balance. When I was sure he was okay, I reached for him.

Fisting a hand in his hair, I brought his head to my breast. "Suck on me. Hard."

He immediately took my left nipple into his mouth, using his tongue to work the tip into a taut point. He seemed to know instinctively how much pressure to use, and when he scraped his teeth over me, it brought a ragged cry to my lips.

He paused, eyes flicking up to my face.

I brought the crop down on his ass, hard enough to sting, but not to hurt. "I didn't tell you to stop."

He went back to the task at hand with as much enthusiasm

as before, this time alternating between my breasts. After a few minutes, his talented mouth had me aching and ready.

"Sit down." I gestured to the space in front of me.

He moved with easy fluidity and I took another moment to admire him before I grabbed the condom I'd gotten ready earlier. Tearing it open, I leaned forward and slowly rolled it over his thick shaft. My knuckles brushed against his stomach, the tense muscles twitching under my touch.

"Are you enjoying yourself?" I asked softly.

"Yes." His voice was a low, husky rasp and the gleam of satisfaction in his eyes made me smile.

"Good." I trailed my fingers down his thigh. "That's good, Jack. Now you get to show me how much you appreciated it."

I moved to straddle his lap, but didn't sink down on him. Not yet. He was strung far too tight. No matter how much control he had, I doubted he'd be able to overcome his body's natural needs if I slid down on him right now. I pushed my hands through his hair, making slow, even strokes across his scalp until I felt the tension in his body start to ease.

"Now, Jack, are you ready to show me how much you appreciated it?"

"Hell, yes," Jack said and the words were ragged, underscored with an unspoken demand. He didn't say it, but I knew he was almost dying for release.

I was, too.

Smiling at him, I finally lowered myself enough for contact, brushing the tip of him against me. His latex-sheathed dick felt good, and I shivered in appreciation. He was hot. His cock was average size, but he was thicker than normal, and I knew he would feel amazing stretching me.

Taking his hands, I guided them to my hips. I was the one calling the shots, so I was at least going to get at least one thing I wanted.

Oblivion.

"I want you to fuck me now, Jack. Hard."

I put my hands on his shoulders as I dropped a bit lower. We both moaned. My hands flexed on his shoulders, nails digging into his flesh.

"I want to feel it in the morning. Got it?"

His eyes widened slightly, pupils spiking. Something flashed across his face and then a slow smile curled his lips. "Yes, ma'am."

"Any rules?"

"Yes. You don't stop, and you don't get to come until I do."

He nodded and his grip on my hips tightened. He raised his hips even as he pulled me down, driving himself deep and hard. My head fell back and Jack began to prove that he was a man of many talents.

---

AS HE DRESSED, Jack asked if he could see me again. I gave him a noncommittal shrug. I wasn't totally opposed to the idea. I had to admit, he was the best partner I'd had in a good long while. He was definitely the best sub I'd ever topped. And he was an all-around good guy from what I saw.

On my way to the front of the club, my body ached in all the best ways and I knew that I'd be able to sleep better than I had in a while. He'd done exactly as I'd asked, fucked me good and hard, and all the stress that had been caged inside me had drifted away with each climax.

He hadn't just held back until I came. He'd held back until I came *twice*.

Jack wasn't a novice, or somebody looking to hold his hand, either. He was doing the same thing I was, looking for a partner.

Someone who got everything he needed. If he'd been a switch, the two of us would've been perfect for each other.

But he was a sub through and through, and in the end, I needed more.

Still, I wasn't against the idea of us hooking up again in the future, and that had been what I told him. He'd taken my lack of commitment with good-natured humor and kissed me gently. Proving again what a great guy he was.

And then, right before he'd left, he said, "It can't be easy."

I'd looked at him in confusion and he just shrugged.

"It can be a bitch sometimes, finding a decent partner. I'm sure you've heard it. I'm not a submissive guy outside of here, but when it comes to sex...well, all I want is to please the woman I'm with, and I enjoy submitting. Finding a partner who gets that can be complicated. I've been with more than a couple of female Doms who deal with the same sort of crap, just the opposite side of the coin. The guy is supposed to be on top and the woman is supposed to submit. All that shit. I figured you probably got it too, except from both ends."

"How'd you know?" I'd asked, curious. Nobody ever figured out that I was a switch, unless I told them. And I didn't make a practice of that. In the bdsm world, being a switch was almost like how some people looked at being bisexual. That you could only be one or the other. Both was somehow confused. Not everyone thought like that, not even the majority, I thought, but I still always kept it to myself.

"It wasn't hard, Dena." His eyes had roamed over me appreciatively and then he'd given me a smile before turning back to the door. "A good partner picks up on what the other one wants or needs. Same way you did with me." He'd opened the door then, and looked over his shoulder. "If you're ever in the mood, look me up."

## THREE

## ARIK

Music blasted around me as I stepped into the club, but it wasn't so loud that I couldn't hear myself think. I took that as a good sign. This was only my second visit to Club Privé since moving to New York. So far I hadn't decided on whether or not I wanted to join, but so far, things were looking good.

I was greeted by one of the hostesses, and she led me up to the VIP floor. She hadn't asked for my name, but she'd greeted me with it. I assumed that meant she remembered me from my initial visits here. That was service for you. But that was also why they had a VIP section, and why they charged buckets for it.

I'd been places where their VIP section was a joke, but here, it seemed to be worth it. I was moving through the scattering of bodies on the top floor when a good-looking couple approached. After a moment, I put a name to the man's face.

"Gavin, right?" I held out my hand. "The owner?"

"Yes. And you're Arik. Arik Porter, if I remember correctly."

I nodded, not elaborating any further. It was a habit. I only gave the needed information, never anything more.

"What do you think of my club?"

I gave him a noncommittal smile and nodded to the woman with him, a gorgeous blonde who he clearly adored.

She held out her hand. "I'm Carrie. I hope you're enjoying yourself."

"Right now, I'm just looking to get a drink and sit down for a little while." I hadn't decided on anything beyond that, although I hoped to scout the group out and see if I couldn't find somebody to...keep me company.

Carrie smiled brightly. "Well, let's get that taken care of. Would you care to join us?"

It seemed like as good a plan as any to get the lay of the land, so I nodded. A few minutes later, I found myself sitting at a table with them, a drink in hand while Gavin, Carrie and I chatted easily.

"What brings you to New York?" Carrie asked, tossing her golden curls over her shoulder. "You mentioned that you were new to the city?"

I nodded. She wasn't a native either, judging by the slight Southern drawl. "I was offered a new job, and it was worth the move."

I didn't offer anything more, and Gavin moved the conversation in a different direction. He asked if I'd belonged to any clubs back home, mentioning that he had briefly thought of expanding into other cities. When I said I was from Chicago, Carrie immediately mentioned that her best friend was originally from the windy city, and the conversation meandered from there.

After nearly twenty minutes, Carrie excused herself to go talk to someone she knew, and a short while after that, somebody came to haul Gavin away on business relating to the club. He told me to enjoy myself and let him know if I needed anything. I assured him I would.

I had to admit that even though I enjoyed talking to them

both, I wasn't sorry to see them go. I hadn't come to make conversation, and now that I'd had my drink, I was ready to find a distraction. That wasn't the sort of thing I wanted to do with an audience.

As I made my way to the stairs, a cute redhead bumped into me. She looked up at me from under her lashes, offering a giggling apology that suited her youthful appearance.

I smiled, but before I could brush around her, she moved closer and rested a hand against my chest. A bold move for someone I immediately marked as a submissive. Then again, she might've been the kind of sub who liked to flirt and push until she finally found someone to punish her.

"Are you...looking for anybody particular?" she asked, her gaze flicking to my mouth.

"I might be."

She bit her lower lip and slid the hand on my chest down. I caught it before it reached my belt, but I didn't move her away. I was curious to see what she'd do next. I wasn't opposed to delivering a little bit of punishment at the moment.

"I can be anybody. Somebody." She licked her lips again and moved in closer. "Nobody. Take your pick."

I let my eyes run down her body. She was about average height, slender, and wearing a few strips of silk and lace that barely covered her essentials. She was beautiful, and I had a feeling she'd do every single thing I told her.

Wrap those cherry-red lips around my cock and suck. Let me fuck her mouth.

Spank her ass until it was hot and pink, my hand stinging.

Use a flogger. A crop. Any one of the dozens of toys I was sure the club provided their VIP patrons.

Fuck her in every position possible. In her pussy. In her ass. As hard and as fast as I wanted.

Make her scream my name, and beg me to let her come.

I knew she would let me do all of that and more. All I had to do was say the word, and she'd be mine for however long it took for us both to be sated.

My gaze came back to her face. "So, anybody. Somebody. Nobody. Do you have an actual name I should call you?"

# FOUR

## DENA

I'd expected to be nervous. After all, this was the job I'd been working toward my whole life, so it made sense that my stomach felt like it had butterflies as I walked into the Manhattan DA's office. The offices were huge and not a little intimidating, but I had my game face on and didn't let the nerves show.

Dressed in what I considered my best power suit, I crossed the black and white tiled floor with slow deliberation, my briefcase swinging from my hand and my head held high. I'd spent hours yesterday picking out exactly what I wanted to wear this morning.

The pinstripe two-piece suit fit me to perfection. The pencil skirt stopped at my knee and the fitted jacket stopped just a little below my waist. I wore a white camisole under it that displayed a hint of lace at vee of the double breasted bodice. It was feminine and flattering, but understated and more powerful for it.

My shoes, on the other hand, were anything but understated.

They were murder red Manolo Blahniks – my favorite shoes.

They matched the bag I carried and I know both the bag and the shoes made a statement, but it wasn't as much about the statement as it was about me personally. I liked how the entire outfit made me feel, and today, I needed that. I needed to feel like I was a woman to be taken seriously and not a child to be overlooked.

As planned, I arrived five minutes early and took a few moments to look around. Despite the power suit and kick-ass shoes, I felt out of place, and started to worry that I looked out of place too.

I mentally chided myself. I wouldn't be here if I didn't belong, if I couldn't do the job I was assigned to do. I belonged here just as much as anybody else and I knew that. At least most of me did.

"Well," a low voice said, drawing the word out. "Hello there."

Even before I turned around, I knew what I was going to find. Years of experience had already taught me this lesson. I deliberately waited a beat before turning to meet a set of turquoise eyes set in the face of a man who could only be described as pretty. And judging by the look on his face, he knew it too. Every inch of him said he spent more time in front of the mirror than I did.

His gaze slithered over me, and I set my face into an expression of cool disdain. He was smiling, although the smile wasn't directed at me. How could it be? He was too busy checking out my rack and my legs.

I cleared my throat and waited for his gaze to swing upward. When it did, I gave an icy smile. A practiced mask settled on his face, one I recognized. I was supposed to be charmed or flattered by his clearly appreciative perusal.

I didn't blink, holding his gaze until he looked away first.

Still, he didn't look the least bit embarrassed or ashamed. As he stepped forward, he held out a hand.

"I'm Pierce Lawton, the new ADA. Would you by chance be...ah, Dena, I believe? The other one?"

The other one. Nice. "Yes. Dena Monroe." I took his hand and gave him a short, quick shake, long enough for him to know he hadn't intimidated me, but too short for him to read into it.

"I don't know about you, but I'm looking forward to diving in. Getting my hands dirty." He gave me a quick wink that I was sure he thought was charming. "It's okay to be nervous, you know. Between the defense attorneys and the scum they represent, it's hard to know who's sleazier."

I had an answer to that question, but kept it to myself. A moment later, I was glad I had.

A woman strode in, pausing only briefly when she saw us. Sharp blue eyes moved from Pierce to me, and then she nodded. "Good," she said, her voice crisp. "You're both here. Follow me."

She didn't introduce herself, but I had to assume she was Bethany McDermott, the ADA I was told I'd be working with. She looked to be in her mid-forties, but with plenty of make-up and her honey-blonde curls professionally done, she might've been older. When she walked into an office, I saw her name on the door, confirming her identity.

She strode around the desk and only then turned to face us. Bracing her hands on the desk, she studied us for a moment. She wore her own version of a power suit. It was the same sapphire color as her eyes, and close-fitting, flattering her lush curves without being obvious.

She looked like the kind of woman who drank souls and had the hearts of her victims for breakfast.

"Okay, so this is how it's going to work. Due to our current situation, we aren't going to do our usual six-week training period. I don't have time to coddle or baby either of you. Figure out how to swim, or you're out. Be prepared to learn and learn fast. We hired you because we assumed you could do the job without us having to hold your hand along the way." She paused, her eyes sliding over to me. "Will that be a problem?"

My spine stiffened as her gaze locked with mine. It felt like I was getting singled out, and I didn't care for it. But I didn't let my reaction show. "Of course not."

She flicked a look at Pierce and arched one perfectly plucked eyebrow.

"That's how I work." He gave her the same slow, smug smile he'd given me earlier.

I resisted the urge to roll my eyes, but just barely. What a schmuck. But every office, firm, classroom, had a guy like him, if not two or three. I learned how to deal with them years ago, and generally it was best to ignore.

"Good." She pushed a button on her phone and when a voice came on, she said, "Darcy, I wanted those files now." She looked up at us again. "I've got a lot of cases on my desk, and basically, the two of you are going to do all of the scut work I don't trust to the paralegals. You won't say a word to a judge until I've determined you won't fuck up my cases." She gave me a condescending smile. "Is language an issue for either of you?"

I had a few choice words I wouldn't have minded sharing with her.

"Of course not." I smiled blandly.

"Excellent." She gave a short nod as the door swung open and a rather harried young woman stuck her head in. "Bring in the case files."

While Bethany addressed the person I assumed was Darcy, I mentally sighed over the fact that I was back to being the bottom rung on the totem pole. Part of me had anticipated it, but it was still grating. I might not have argued criminal cases before, but I'd been presenting to judges on my own for a couple of years.

As Darcy stepped out again, Bethany turned back to Pierce and me. "As you've probably figured out, I'm your direct supervisor, which means I'll be deciding if and when you're ready to take on cases of your own. You do a good job and I'll get you into the court room. Screw me over and you'll be lucky to argue shit in traffic court."

Darcy shuffled in with an overflowing file box, looking like she could barely hold on. I was petite, but this skinny wisp of a woman looked like she was about to fall over. Instinctively, I moved to help, taking it from her as I glanced toward Pierce, waiting for him to step in.

He didn't, solidifying my opinion of him as a total asshole.

"Thanks for taking the initiative, Dena." Bethany gave me a cool smile. "There's a list in there that details everything I need. I also had Darcy send it to your email so there aren't any excuses. Pierce, you're with me."

The box gouged my hips with its sharp corners as Bethany strode out of the office, Pierce at her heels. Staring at their backs, I briefly imagined giving into the childish urge to stick my tongue out at them. I didn't, of course, but it would've been satisfying.

"You have an office." Darcy gave me a small, nervous smile when I looked at her.

"Excuse me?"

"You already have a space to work. I'm not sure I'd call it an office, but it's yours."

I nodded and grimly tightened my grip on the box. "Lead the way."

SOME NINE PLUS HOURS LATER, I collapsed face-down on the couch in my apartment, more thankful than ever that I didn't have a roommate. I had a sweet little place in Chelsea, and it was my pride and joy. Just then, though, I couldn't take the time to appreciate the restored brick walls or the view, or anything else for that matter.

All I wanted was peace and quiet, and maybe in a little while, a glass of wine.

Fuck that. I might just have the whole damn bottle.

My first day as an ADA hadn't exactly been what I could call glamorous. It hadn't been exciting. I couldn't really even say it had been fulfilling. I could have handled the lack of glamour and excitement. Those stars had been wiped from my eyes a long time ago. But it would have been nice if the day hadn't completely sucked.

Once Darcy had shown me into my office – it was hardly more than a closet – I had spent the first hour dealing with a computer that had come straight out of the Stone Age.

Then I'd spent several hours going blind on legal briefs. There were filings and reports, things that were generally handled by paralegals. Except Bethany didn't seem to have any paralegals around. I knew things were tight since they'd let Pierce and I slide on the usual training, but it still seemed excessive.

Then again, my boss seemed like that kind of person. Excessive. And not in a generous kind of way. When I'd been coming back from lunch, Bethany had found me and demanded to know how far I'd gotten.

"You're not done yet?" she'd snapped. Then with a shake of her head, she'd shoved a clipboard into my hands. "People up for parole. I argued the cases in court. Write the letters. You can pull up the details on your computer."

I'd seen the conference table through the glass behind her,

and both she and Pierce had looked to be working on something else, something that apparently required them to have meals brought in. Rather than ask why he was working with her rather than me, I simply nodded end and retreated to my cell. My office.

And that was where I'd stayed until I'd realized it was after five. When I left, I saw Pierce coming out of an office a few doors down from Bethany's. I'd managed to catch a glimpse into the room before he shut the door completely.

"My new office." He'd given me a smug smile. "You like yours?"

"It suits me just fine," I'd lied.

I wasn't a superficial person, but I did believe in equality and fairness. Two people starting out the same should be treated the same. There was no reason for Pierce's office to be an actual office, with room for a real desk and some movement. But there it was.

Now, I was lying on my couch and trying not to brood too much. It didn't mean anything. Maybe he actually had more experience than I did. I was pretty sure he was nearly a decade older. Maybe he'd transferred from another DA's office, and he had more seniority. It didn't matter.

That was what I told myself. I didn't particularly believe it, though. The phone rang, but I ignored it. I didn't want to talk to anyone, didn't want to deal with anyone asking me how things had gone, didn't want to have to listen to anyone else talk about their problems. I just wanted to be left alone.

I ignored pretty much everything right up until my bladder forced me off the couch and into the bathroom. I could see the screen of my phone showing that I had messages, but I didn't answer any of them. I didn't even look at them.

What I did do was get myself something to drink.

After pouring myself a glass of wine, I retreated into my bathroom and settled down for a nice long soak.

"Tomorrow will be better," I said. Relaxing back into my lavender and vanilla bubbles, I sighed. "Tomorrow will be better."

---

WHAT A LINE OF BULLSHIT.

The next day wasn't any better, nor were the days that followed. I felt like I was an associate all over again, and it annoyed the crap out of me.

It only got worse on Wednesday morning when I took some files to Bethany's office. I paused in the doorway, listening while Pierce explained a tact he would have tried if he was first chair on some case they were working on.

I stood there stiffly, my hands gripping the files I held, waiting for them to notice me. When they finished, Pierce glanced over at me and gave me a surprised look as if he'd just now realized I was there. Bethany, however, eyed me dismissively before going back to the notes she was working on.

"Did you need something?" Pierce asked.

"I just need to give Bethany the research notes she needed." Keeping my voice level, I walked across the floor and put everything down. As I was turning away, I heard papers rustling.

"Oh, great. I needed this for that filing I was doing for you, Bethany."

I stiffened even more, one hand curling into a fist. Unlike a lot of lawyers, I didn't thrive on conflict. In fact, I didn't even really like it. I liked making logical arguments, presenting clear and concise evidence.

But a girl could only take so much for so long, and I was heading down that path.

I was being jerked around and I knew it. I'd need to address it, but I wouldn't do it without thinking things through. This wasn't some asshole at a club. This was my job, the place that I'd always dreamed of being. I wasn't going to lose that in a moment of rash temper. No matter how justified.

But just as I reached the door, Bethany spoke, "Actually, Dena, it's a good thing you stopped by. It saves me from having to hunt you down later."

I turned toward her, letting her know I was listening.

"I've been given the okay to put the two of you up for the next case that comes across my desk. You'll be taking second chair, of course. I'll be arguing the case, but you'll be there to see how things work."

I blinked, almost certain I'd heard wrong. Pierce grinned as he shoved his hands into his pockets. Bethany ignored him, her pen scratching across the surface of her notepad.

"In the meantime, I'm presenting you two with a case. It's already been closed, but I want to hear strategies on how you would've handled it had you been trying it." Now she looked up, sliding her gaze from Pierce to me. "Consider this trial by fire. Don't fuck up."

Something hot and pleased settled inside me.

Pierce glanced at me, but I didn't waste my time looking at him now.

Trials by fire suited me just fine.

**End of preview.**
**The Club Privé series continues in *Unlawful Attraction (Club Privé Book 7)*, available now.**

# ABOUT THE AUTHOR

M. S. Parker is a USA Today Bestselling author and the author of the Erotic Romance series, Club Privè and Chasing Perfection.

Living in Las Vegas, she enjoys sitting by the pool with her laptop writing on her next spicy romance.

Growing up all she wanted to be was a dancer, actor or author. So far only the latter has come true but M. S. Parker hasn't retired her dancing shoes just yet. She is still waiting for the call for her to appear on Dancing With The Stars.

When M. S. isn't writing, she can usually be found reading–oops, scratch that! She is always writing.

*For more information:*
www.msparker.com
msparkerbooks@gmail.com

 facebook.com/msparkerauthor

# ACKNOWLEDGMENTS

First, I would like to thank all of my readers. Without you, my books would not exist. I truly appreciate each and every one of you.

A big "thanks" goes out to all the Facebook fans, street team, beta readers, and advanced reviewers. You are a HUGE part of the success of all my series.

I have to thank my PA, Shannon Hunt. Without you my life would be a complete and utter mess. Also a big thank you goes out to my editor Lynette and my wonderful cover designer, Sinisa. You make my ideas and writing look so good.

Made in the USA
Monee, IL
12 May 2021